K83
BKM
No good! good!
VM

NEWARK PUBLIC LIBRARY
W9-BPP-368
00006 0989

DW

...AWN

BH

DUE IN 7 DAYS
14 DAY LOAN

Newark Public Library
BOOKMOBILE

THE
NEW MEXICO
HERITAGE

Also by Lauran Paine
In Thorndike Large Print

THE HORSEMAN
THE HOMESTEADERS
THE MARSHAL
SKYE
TANNER

THE
NEW MEXICO
HERITAGE

Lauran Paine

THORNDIKE PRESS • THORNDIKE, MAINE

Library of Congress Cataloging in Publication Data:

Paine, Lauran.
   The New Mexico heritage/Lauran Paine. p. cm.
   ISBN 0-89621-826-0 (lg. print: alk. paper)
   1. Large type books. I. Title.
   [PS3566.A34N4 1987b]   813'.54—dc19

                                        87-16117
                                        CIP

Copyright © 1987 by Lauran Paine. All rights reserved.

Large Print edition available by arrangement with Walker and
Company, New York.
All the characters and events portrayed in this story are fictitious.

Cover design by Bernie Beckman.

THE
NEW MEXICO
HERITAGE

783082

788082

CHAPTER 1

MARIA ANTONIA GALLEGOS LORD

The Hopis owned it, the Navajos took it from them. In the autumn of the Navajo's flowering, sixteen Texans rode for a lean strippling named David Lord, whose mother had called him Bluebonnet because of the color of his eyes. They drove four hundred unpredictable, razor-back, wicked-horned cattle into the sweet-grass country claimed by the Tribal Council. As Lord's slab-sided fighting cattle fanned out, the Texans established their basic cow camp along a warm-water creek of the New Mexico Territory they called the Little Snake for its crookedness. They erected three adobe structures with walls three feet thick, kept one man atop a flat roof watching for Indians, and settled in.

As David Lord told it many years later, when he was still lean and hard-eyed but older and supposedly more tolerant and mellow, when the Indians quit wrangling among themselves about a course of action and rode to battle against what their neighbors, the Apaches, called the *pind-o-lick-o-yees*, or "white-eyes," he and his Texans were ready.

The scattered Navajo gunfire got no response from the forted-up Texans. Emboldened by this, the Navajos had harangued themselves into a real fighting mood rather than a sniping mood, and mounted a headlong horseback attack.

The Texans waited until they could not miss, then fired three coordinated volleys from behind their thick mud walls. The smoke rose slowly; dead Indians and horses were everywhere. It was, Dave Lord recalled, the most terrible view he had ever looked upon, and that included nine slaughter-field battles he had participated in during the Civil War.

The Indians did not return in force, but later they sniped at Lord's Texans, killing four, and they killed almost half his Longhorns. They caught Dave one time in a mesquite ambush, shot the horse from under him, broke his left arm, and shot him through the right thigh.

In retaliation, Lord sold a hundred of his cattle four months later, used the money to hire seven renegade army deserters, took plenty of time organizing things, and one hour before sunrise struck a big rancheria nineteen miles south of his fort-camp. When they were finished they rode home without a single casualty, leaving death and devastation on both sides of lower Little Snake Creek.

What probably would have become a drawn-out war of attrition was scotched when the army came into the territory for the purpose of enforcing order. Two Indian ambushes of soldier-patrols ended up in a full-scale campaign including the use of cannon, cavalry, Gatling guns, and finally, the slaughter of all Navajo livestock the army could find.

Dave Lord borrowed money, restocked his grass country, replaced most of his Texans — all of them, over a period of years — with others, and by working eighteen hours a day, year in and year out, prospered, marginally at first, more so later. By the time he married and started a family, David Lord's unshakable resolve had made him a man of considerable wealth and substance. He claimed all the territory his cattle and horses grazed over, thousands of acres of good to middling New Mexico land. And unlike so many of his kind, he made the transition from a gunfighting buckskin buccaneer to a patriarch with little difficulty, overseeing thousands of head of livestock that roamed over hundreds of miles of land.

He and his wife, the daughter of a cattle *patrón* named Severino Gallegos, had four children. But on the clear, beautiful day when dozens of people stood bareheaded out at the ranch cemetery to hear last rites for old David Lord, only one heir remained; a tall daughter with dark hair and eyes, a complexion like pale gold, and a jaw of granite. She was at the time of her father's passing thirty-one years old, unmarried, absolutely capable, and, so it was said, cold.

The impressively ritualized ceremony for the late David Lord was performed by Father O'Malley from Mission San Buenaventura. The dilapidated old mission school and church were on the outskirts of the nearest town (earlier known as Tanque Verde, now known as Lordsville) and had been supported almost exclusively by non-Catholic David Lord and his very devout wife Anjelica. After the ceremony, Father O'Malley went to stand beside Maria Antonia Gallegos Lord, the tall, very reserved, and beautiful new owner of Lord's Land, as the huge ranch was called.

There had been a large assemblage of mourners. David Lord had died the patrón of hundreds of local people, mostly of Mexican descent. His earlier exploits fifty years ago, far from being recalled as piracy, had grown into heroic legend — for everyone except the Navajos. But what they passed down from generation to generation was spoken in a language non-Navajos neither used nor understood.

As the crowd dispersed, most passing in front of Maria Antonia wearing sorrow and condolence on their faces, a few bold ones spoke softly in Spanish. One or two of the women even dared to touch her hand or arm as the good father looked straight ahead, his blue eyes upon the men filling in the grave.

It was early spring. The searing heat which was to come would not arrive for another six or eight weeks, for which Father O'Malley was grateful, because he would have been uncomfortably warm in his robe and full vestments, even with cottonwood shade over the ranch's private cemetery. Perhaps after nine years at Mission San Buenaventura Father O'Malley should have adapted more than he had, especially since prior to coming here he had lived nine years on the South Desert. But before that he had lived thirty-nine years in the place of his birth, New York City.

When the buggies and saddle horses were stirring light dust on their way back to town or to the other places they had come from — such

11

as distant adjoining ranches, and even the mud cubes called *jacals* of the very humble people — Father O'Malley removed his stole and loosened his collar. He turned his pale blue eyes toward the handsome woman who still stood like a statue: erect, impassive, distant, and in Father O'Malley's eyes, magnificent.

In Spanish he said, "Rest tranquil, Maria Antonia, the Lord is your shepherd." He added in English, "The responsibility is now yours. You will use it wisely." Father O'Malley paused as a very brief but sharp reflection of blinding sunlight off metal made him squint in the direction of a distant knoll, where several trees stood. Then he said, "May God grant you grace along with wisdom — and Maria Antonia, be tough."

She was turning her head to speak when she abruptly staggered, and fell. At the same instant a gunshot echoed from nearby.

The men working at the grave were astonished into immobility. So was Father O'Malley, but he recovered quickly and dropped to her side. He saw the blood and reacted to it by shouting for the men to run for help. As they stood in dumb incomprehension he yelled. "Damn you — *do it!* Go to the house, bring a wagon, bring help. *Go! Andele!*"

They dropped shovels and fled in several

directions as Father O'Malley eased Maria Antonia onto her back, bending low to loosen the uppermost of the two dozen black buttons down the front of her dress.

Blood gushed. There was no ebbing as a torrent of scarlet flowed in cadence with each heartbeat. Father O'Malley used a clean handkerchief from a cassock pocket to wipe blood from the wound, and before it gushed again he saw the hole. It was small, with very little ragged flesh around its puckered edges. He prayed hard as he worked to stanch the flow of blood.

There were two holes. The one in back where the bullet exited was the worst, although the bullet had obviously not been solid lead, which would have fragmented when it struck. Joseph Henry O'Malley had encountered bullet wounds before on the South Desert. Quite a few in fact, so he was not a novice at what he now attempted to do. In his experience, however, when injuries were as bad as this one, few things helped.

But Father O'Malley was a stubborn man. Last rites could wait. He felt certain that before long they would be required, but until then he mopped blood and called upon his knowledge of the human body to speculate on what damage had been done and which means to stop the bleeding might prove effective.

The sun was moving, more shade speckled the area, and flies began to appear. Most noticeable of all was the utter silence. He looked in the direction of the ranch buildings. There was frantic activity back there, but thus far no sign of a wagon to take Maria Antonia to the sprawling hacienda with its courtly enclosed patio, its many spacious, cool and sparsely furnished rooms.

He did all he knew to do, then he prayed, and the bleeding seemed to be diminishing. Father O'Malley, who had been the only son of a hod-carrying Irish immigrant, had grown to manhood in the toughest part of old New York. By the time he had succumbed to the call to serve, he had developed a healthy skepticism. He still had it, and while he never denied the possibility of miracles and the power of prayer, now as he leaned down closer to assure himself that the bleeding was indeed lessening, the vestiges of his secular nature inclined him to suspect that while his praying might be responsible, it was equally possible that the human body, which normally reacts to shock by shutting down some of its functions, was performing this act now.

He heard the wagon coming. There were at least a dozen people of both sexes trotting along on both sides of it. He could hear an occasional lamentation over the rattling of the wagon.

He tore black cloth from Maria Antonia's dress from which to make dry compresses. She was waxen and inert. He maneuvered his thick body to shade her eyes from the shafts of sunlight coming down unmercifully through the tree-tops.

He was watching the oncoming entourage and did not see her open both eyes and look directly up at him. By the time he glanced down her eyes were closed again.

He tried to clean his hands. Her blood was also on his robe, and patches were drying darkly on the ground. He waved the flies away and watched her shallow breathing, which was fluttery and uneven. There was even less blood oozing from her wounds now, but as Father O'Malley knew, this was perhaps not the blessing it looked to be. People shot through the upper body more often than not had at least one collapsed lung, and internal bleeding.

The wagon reached an iron gate, where its driver hauled around, and backed his rig as close as he could. Father O'Malley rose to watch the people pour through the gate, and he held up a hand as several grief-sticken Mexican women would have hurled themselves on the ground beside Maria Antonia. "No," he exclaimed. "Bring a blanket. It must be put under her. She must not be allowed to bend, the blanket must be kept taut. Here, four men on each side."

"She is dead. Holy Mother, they have killed her!" someone cried out.

"No, she lives," exclaimed the priest, shooing the women out of the way as the men brought an old brown blanket from the wagon. "Please, go back a little. Hear me, please, do not crowd close. She lives, be assured that she lives. Now, be very careful with the lifting. Very careful."

CHAPTER 2

A YOUNG DOCTOR, AN OLD DOCTOR

Old David Lord had tried with absolutely no success to limit the size of his ranch yard. In other areas, where there was no lingering trace of feudalism, this was possible. In Montana, Wyoming, Colorado, single rangemen lived as Spartans in bunkhouses, going to town on Saturday nights to let loose. They drifted like autumn leaves.

Where Spanish influence had established mores, riders were not drifters, and they rarely went to town to drink and play poker. They were family men and belonged to the land, to their families, to the founders and descendants of the founders of the great ranches. They had adobe homes on the ranch, usually not far from the great yard, which was the center of their lives, of their universe. When they were cow-

17

boys instead of *vaqueros,* they adapted if they were able, or they rode on if they could not.

The yard of the Lord Ranch sprawled over twenty acres. It always smelled of cooking. There, children played, and women scolded, birthed babies, buried the old and the young who could not survive. Almost any season of the year someone wore black, or someone else got married. It was a community unto itself, a world whose overseer was *el patrón.* The things which mattered in this part of the country were the faith, the family, the ranch.

For two days after the shooting, people from all around came to the Lord house. A few were admitted, but very few. The others said their beads on the cool, secluded patio, or beyond it, where dust lay in soft layers. Children were silenced, people worked solemnly, watching rigs and riders arrive from Lordsville. Conversation was fragmentary and interspersed with long silences. El Patrón's daughter was dying. Who had done such a thing? And when she died, what would become of everyone? She had no heir. When this had happened elsewhere almost invariably the *gringos* had become owners, and they had a totally different method of cattle ranching. It did not include married range-riders, fiestas, religious ceremonies. Cattle were not driven in by the dozen to be butchered and divided among the families.

It was a very busy time for Father O'Malley. He understood the fears exactly, and while he could sympathize he could not predict what would happen, and that limited the reassurances he could offer in good conscience.

Lordsville's physician of many years was Dr. Homer Hudspeth. He had been a Union surgeon during the war. Since then, he had competently set broken bones and done minor surgery. Recently he had taken in a much younger man as his associate. And as failing eyesight increasingly limited his activities, he had taken up drinking whiskey, something his associate physician disapproved of but said very little about, reasoning that when a man was eighty years old with failing eyesight, what possible harm could the whiskey do before his time ran out?

Dr. Hudspeth and his associate were both summoned to the Lord ranch the day Maria Antonia had been shot, and they returned each day thereafter. On one buggy ride back to town, Dr. Hudspeth had offered his private opinion to Dr. George Brunner that Maria Antonia could not possibly live, and the only thing that had kept her breathing this long was a heritage of fierce determination, plus the Texas hardiness she had inherited from old David Lord.

As they were putting up the rig Homer Hudspeth paused to look over the mare's back at the younger man. "George," he said, "her father had enough scars for three men. I knew him very well. I would have been out there at the cemetery except for a confounded attack of the tremors. . . . That woman is old David's spittin' image. Maybe not in coloring, but in every other way. She'll resist right up until her heart stops."

The younger man, who was sandy-haired and gray-eyed, lean and of average height, returned the older man's gaze as he said, "Every day improves her chances. I wouldn't have bet a plugged centavo on her surviving that first day. Homer, this morning she looked — she even had some color in her cheeks. She looked —"

"George, you are young. I was young once, and idealistic and full of zeal — among other things. . . . You finish up here. I've got to get up to the house."

Dr. Brunner watched the older man's swift hike toward the rear of the house they shared wagging his head. Then he corraled the mare, parked the top-buggy, pitched the driving harness onto the floorboards in front of the single seat, and dropped down upon an old horseshoe keg to enjoy some silence and shade.

He was a vigorous man, thirty-five years old.

He needed knowledge the way vaqueros needed horses. He was a handsome man, who did not look muscular but who was. It had taken him four years of study and two years after that to find his niche. And now that he had found it, he remained as restless as he had felt before finding it. He had grown up in Nebraska, which was also cattle country, but such a different kind of cattle country from this New Mexico Territory. He was still struggling to overcome preconceived notions and to decide whether or not to adapt to this place where his present medical practice was located.

He had encountered degrees of superstition on the South Desert he had been unprepared to believe still existed anywhere in the world. Old Homer had laughed at George's red-faced frustration at being called to treat natives whose first choice had been *curanderas,* old women whose treatments included disemboweled chickens and yucca root poultices.

The sounds of Lordsville reached faintly into the shed. Someone was shaping steel over an anvil, someone else was driving nails, a dog-fight erupted. The fight was accompanied by loud cheers, and profanity in English and Spanish. It ended with howling, as someone kicked one of the dogs. The air smelled of heavily spiced cooking, and behind all this was a faint echo of guitar music; someone was singing a dolorous Spanish ballad of lost love and early death. George Brunner wagged his head again; these people were so miserably fatalistic.

He left the cool shed, washed in the kitchen of the old house, which smelled faintly of carbolic acid even when all the windows were open, and listened to a pair of masculine voices speaking low in the parlor. Homer had a patient – or one of his drinking friends – out there.

As George opened the rear door to fling out the basin of dirty water, Homer called his name. He hung the basin from its nail, running one hand through his hair as he headed for the parlor.

Homer was wearing his steel-framed glasses, which meant to George that it was a patient with him. The other man was burned a mahogany color from exposure, but he had blue eyes and curly, too long fair hair. In general appearance he was lanky, faded and weathered. He wore a belt gun with an ivory handle, and when George came into the room the man looked up at him from a slightly hawkish face.

Homer was sitting so close his knees touched the knees of his patient. He was working with knitted brows over a mean gash in the lanky man's lower left arm. Homer paused to lean back, remove the glasses, and mop irritably at his eyes, which invariably watered when he did close work. Then he looked over his shoulder at George. "Horseshoe nail," he said. "It's a poor week when there isn't at least one rip from them. George, this is Mr. Barnard. Mr. Barnard, this is my associate, Dr. Brunner. George Brunner." Having performed this service, Dr. Hudspeth struggled up out of his chair. "I've got it cleaned, George." He nodded to the lanky man and headed for the kitchen, where his bottles were arranged in soldierly ranks in a wall cupboard.

George nodded, sat down, and examined the injury.

The lanky man said, "Damn-fool horse yanked his foot away before I could clinch the nails."

George nodded. He found pieces of dirt that had not been removed and, using tweezers, went after them. He did not look up until the wound was ready for disinfecting and bandaging. Then he smiled at the stranger. "This will sting."

The patient inclined his head. "Yeah."

Nothing more was said between them until George was bandaging the arm. The lanky man flexed his fingers. "I got one of these rips in

Nebraska one time. That time it was in the leg, an' I had the horse throwed and tied. He'd never had shoes before. The rope broke. He got me a good one and kicked me in the bargain."

George raised his head. "What part of Nebraska?"

The stranger's eyes grew cold as he looked back. His reply came after a considerable pause, as though it had dawned on him he might be talking to someone from Nebraska. "Sand Hills country," he said shortly, and got to his feet, still flexing his fingers. "How much, Doctor?"

"Half dollar."

The lanky man fished out the coin and dropped it into George's hand. He picked up his hat, nodded brusquely, and walked out into the sunlight.

George went to a window. The lanky man was striding in the direction of the rooming house. George left the silver coin on the table and went back to the kitchen, where Homer was sitting relaxed and slightly flushed. On the table in front of him was a jolt glass and a bottle. Homer looked up with watering eyes. "Did he pay you?" he asked.

"Half dollar. I left it on the table."

"Have a drink, George. Good for what ails you."

George seated himself but ignored the glass and bottle. "Barnard . . . Did he say what his first name was?"

"No. Well, if he did I wasn't listening. Y'know, an awful lot of bad infections come from those nail wounds. It's really no wonder; shoeing horses is filthy work. I've seen 'em get gangrene. Men like that never take care of wounds. They seem to think they are indestructible."

George watched Homer reach to refill his little glass. He waited until the contents had been dropped straight down. "Homer," he said, "we've had a lot of strange ones. I expect because we're so near the border."

Homer nodded as he mopped at his eyes. "I know. And you think this is one of them."

"Well, he mentioned Nebraska, and when I asked what part of it he knew, he pulled back his answer and gave one he probably knew covered a hell of a lot of wild country — the Sand Hills."

Homer shoved the handkerchief back in a coat pocket. Half of it hung out. "So you think he's an outlaw on the run toward the border. Well, he might be, George. He's certainly been in a lot of hot sunshine. He's burned almost as dark as a Mexican. But remember what I told you when you first arrived — never open your mouth to 'em if you got doubts about 'em."

George remembered this bit of wisdom, along with many other bits, and he had conducted himself according to what he knew was good advice. "The town marshal never seems to catch them. I can't remember any being caught in the two years I've been down here," he mused.

The old doctor nodded about that, too. "Now, we don't have to worry about that, do we?" he said, and belched slightly behind an upraised hand. "About Maria Antonia," he went on, changing the subject, "do you mind makin' the call in the morning? I got to — do some accounts and all."

George did not mind. In fact, he had been expecting this since the day after the shooting. Heat and Homer did not work well together. Homer had grown heavier the last couple of years, his breath was short, and while George had his own ideas concerning the cause of those symptoms, there was nevertheless a perfectly good reason for the older man to avoid brilliant sunlight — his eyes.

He left Dr. Hudspeth in the kitchen and went down to the café for an early supper. In Mex Town, behind Lordsville's largely *norteamericano* business district, they had cantinas with better food; at least the taste was better than the stringy steak and mushy potatoes the café man served up with an unvaryingly monotonous regularity in *Gringo* Town.

He paid little attention to the other early diners, of which there were not many, mainly because it was rare to see the same faces at the café man's counter two days in a row unless they were local residents. And unless they were single men, they had the good sense to eat at home.

The marshal was a single man. He was also nearly as broad as he was long, wore a droopy dragoon mustache, had eyes like little gray steel balls, and an insincere smile. He had two gold eyeteeth, which rarely showed unless he really laughed. He also had a burn scar across the back of his left hand. The new skin glistened in sunlight, never having darkened from exposure, and because Marshal Kandelin usually wore gloves, rarely showed.

It did this late afternoon as he ordered his supper, tugging the gloves off before folding them beneath his shell belt. He was graying and could have been forty or fifty, but whatever his age, he had little difficulty maintaining order. He was a man of violent temperament when aroused; otherwise he passed as an ordinary individual with the build of an oak barrel.

He nodded down the counter toward George.

The counter was empty between them. He said, "How's Doña Maria Antonia?"

George stepped eating long enough to reply. "Still with us."

Marshal Kandelin wagged his head and leaned heavily upon the counter. "Did that slug go through her chest?"

"Almost straight through, Marshal, with a slight downward slant. In the front and out the back." George raised his coffee cup and held it motionless for as long as was required for two more customers to walk in and sit at the counter between George and the gorillalike town marshal. Then he drained the cup, rose, dumped coins beside his plate, and left the café, on his way down to the livery barn.

He hired a big, rawboned bay gelding with a long face and deep chest. The liveryman cocked an eye. "If you got a call, Doc, you forgot your satchel."

George smiled. "It's not always necessary."

The liveryman shrugged, not even bothering to watch George leave town by the west-side alley heading across unspoiled grassland as straight as an arrow.

The afternoon was full of light, spreading thin shadows. The sun would not disappear for another two or three hours at this time of the year, but the lower it sank the less heat it seemed capable of producing.

George smelled the ranch yard a half mile before he entered it. There was a faint, fragrant blue haze rising overhead from at least two dozen mud ovens.

He left his horse with a gangling Mexican at the barn and went directly to the main house, where another tall Mexican, this one wearing two six-guns and crossed bandoliers over his chest, carried a Winchester in the crook of one arm. He smiled broadly and held the gate for George to pass through.

George crossed the patio, with its worn and faded handmade tile paving, and paused to knock on a massive, steel-reinforced carved door. When it opened a squatty dark girl with blue and red ribbons braided into her hair smiled and made a slight curtsy before stepping aside.

So far George had not said a word. He followed the girl down a long, domed, white-washed corridor, which was also paved with handmade tiles, but not as faded as the ones outside. She stopped and tapped a closed door, speaking softly in musical Spanish, and George waited for another woman to open it. This one he knew fairly well. The girl with ribbons threw another smile at George as she went past, and he stepped into a very large room with massive wood rafters and every wall white-washed in the traditional way. There was not much furniture; a huge bed with very dark upright posts, a dresser that matched, one mirror encircled in paler wood, which did not seem to belong, and four chairs with seats made of rawhide instead of slats.

The woman who had admitted him hovered near the bed, both hands clasped across a very lean stomach. She was not dark, except for her hair and eyes. She had a high-bridged nose, and a wide mouth with thin lips. Her name was Doña Teresa Maria Gallegos y Meir. She was the aunt and only living relative of the very still and expressionless woman in the bed.

She looked mildly bewildered. "But you were here only this morning, Doctor, and where is your little bag?" she said.

"The little bag," George Brunner explained for the second time this day, "is not always necessary. And yes, indeed, I was here only this morning."

He looked at the woman in the bed, whose very dark eyes had not left his face since he had entered the room. He had always thought, almost wistfully, that Maria Antonia Gallegos Lord was probably the most statuesque and beautiful woman he had ever seen. He still thought so, even now. He turned a chair around and straddled it; then he began asking routine and solicitous questions, most of which Teresa Maria answered so that her niece would not have to. When the courtesies had been disposed of he leaned upon the high back of the chair with his chin on folded arms and asked another question.

"In five days, señorita, there has been considerable talk. In time I am sure you will hear it all, as I have. Señorita, I understand your *mayordomo* and quite a party of vaqueros went out to hunt that man down. They tracked him — or at least tried to track him — and returned pale and worried, because there were no tracks from the hill with the trees."

Maria Antonia gently nodded her head.

"And so they are saying he either had wings or was a phantom, *fantasma,* who disappeared into the air after shooting you."

Tía Teresa Maria, who had been listening keenly with both hands still clasped, said, "Doctor, my niece is very ill and weak. If you came to give medicine or examine the wounds . . ." The clasped hands separated and fluttered like tired birds. "But if not . . . *Si?*"

CHAPTER 3

JUAN ESTEVEN'S IDEA

George respected Tía Teresa Maria, but he had never been able to feel liking for her. Even now, her concern for the beautiful woman in the bed, while selflessly devoted, seemed overly protective.

He looked from the aunt back to the bed. "I am concerned that the ambusher should be caught," he said.

Tía Teresa Maria spoke. "Certainly, Doctor. We all are. Caught and punished."

"Has Marshal Kandelin been out?" he asked the vinegary older woman.

"No. At least, not that I know of. But he may have talked to Juan Esteven."

George nodded about that. Juan Esteven was the mayordomo, the overseer, a position which corresponded to a cow ranch foreman or range boss up north, except that on a ranch as large as the Lord place, an overseer was much more than just a range boss. He and Juan Esteven were good friends, as a result of George having delivered the mayordomo's wife of their fourth son by an extremely difficult breech birth.

George regarded the older woman for a moment of thoughtful silence. She looked directly back from unreadable black eyes set in an expression of prim and forbidding rectitude. He asked if there would be objections to his asking questions, and for the first time the woman in the bed spoke.

"No, no objections at all."

Tía Teresa Maria stepped closer to the bed, frowning, but her niece ignored this. The young woman was regarding Doctor Brunner with interest. "Can you tell me what kind of questions?" she asked in a shallow voice.

George smiled at her. This was not good for her; he would make it brief. "The man who shot you was apparently on that knoll about six hundred yards from the cemetery. I think the distance was very great, even for a rifle. Even for a marksman. And I heard in town that when your vaqueros rode up there, they found no tracks. No shell casing. Nothing at all. I want to ask someone who made that ride to tell me what he saw." He smiled at the beautiful woman. "A fantasma? No, please do not answer." He was rising as he said this. "You asked what my question would be and I've just told you. You couldn't answer it anyway. Maybe Juan Esteven can't either. Thank you. I will be out to change bandages tomorrow. Good day."

He found the dark girl with the ribbons in her hair waiting to let him out of the house. She showed him out onto the patio, where three huge old trees provided shafts of cathedrallike sun-dappled shade year round.

Juan Esteven was sweating profusely, even in the shade of the smithy where he and two younger men were indolently at some chore, which was clearly not critical. Juan came out to meet Dr. Brunner, smiling and shaking his head about the rising heat.

George asked about Juan's wife.

Juan's tawny-brown eyes twinkled. "Fine. She must be, otherwise she would not be screeching at the children and scolding me."

George led the way out of earshot of the youthful vaqueros. He and the mayordomo sat on an old log bench in the shade of a tree. Esteven was a swarthy man of middle height with laugh wrinkles around his eyes. He was a shrewd, capable individual, who had been born on the ranch. He eyed George speculatively and smiled. "My wife will be glad you asked about her. The little boy is now a year and a half old. Are you this solicitous with all your patients, Doctor?"

George grinned. "You are a coyote," he responded. "Juan, when you went up atop that hill where the rifleman was shooting from, what did you find?"

Esteven eyed George pensively for a moment before speaking. "Nothing, amigo. No tracks, no shell casings, no sign of anyone, and from there it is possible to see many miles in all directions." Juan spread his hands, palms downward. "Nothing at all."

George said, "Fantasma?" The overseer laughed. "If so, amigo, his horse must have been one too."

George sat back, squinting out across the huge old dusty yard. Juan Esteven looked at him for a moment. He tapped the doctor's knee. "How could it have happened, then. No?"

"Yes."

The stocky man also leaned back. "Many years ago el patrón and I were over along the base of that hill. Someone said they had seen a mountain lion over there. We found no tracks." Esteven raised and dropped heavy shoulders. "There is always talk. While we were standing with our horses the carpenter who was raising new balks in el patrón's house let one fall. It was a very large timber, half a tree. When it hit the ground it made a great sound." Esteven paused to squint in George's direction. "I don't know how this could be – neither did el patrón – but that sound came all the way over to the hill where we were. It sounded so close we could even hear the log when it bounced and rolled."

The two men sat looking at one another for a long time before George Brunner said, "Would that account for you finding nothing out there the day Maria Teresa was shot?"

Juan Esteven made his helpless hand gesture again. "*Quién sabe, amigo?* Who cay say?" Then his normally good-natured expression changed, grew shrewd. "Because we are good friends I tell you this: Whoever shot our lady was not on that knoll and he was not down along the base of it. Fantasma? Maybe many people do not know better, but you and I do. Fantasmas don't use guns. Maybe they can't lift them, I don't know." Esteven lowered his voice, although there was no one any closer than the shoeing shed, which was well beyond eavesdropping distance. "Compadre, I told no one this, not even the marshal from Lordsville, Kandelin, but I think the rifle shot must have come from the same place that carpenter long ago dropped the big log. It *sounded* like it came from the knoll, but I don't believe that."

George's brow furrowed. He glanced in the direction of the patrón's residence. "From the house?"

Esteven barely inclined his head as he watched Dr. Brunner's expression. "But this is our secret. All right?"

Brunner agreed. "Yes. Juan, when I ride out of the yard I'll go over to the knoll."

Esteven nodded complete understanding. "I will beat on the anvil." He smiled. "You will see."

George settled his hat on his head. "Marshal Kandelin was out here?"

"Once, the day after the shooting. He too went over to the knoll, but I watched, and he did not go up it. He rode along its base on his way back to town."

"But he asked questions?"

"Sí. He talked to some of the people. They told him what they believed — the shot came from the knoll, and afterward the bushwhacker flew away in the air."

"Has the marshal been back, Juan?"

"No. I don't think he will be back, either. But I don't like him, so I would say nothing good about him." Esteven's broad smile brightened up again.

George missed seeing it. He was again peering through sunlight in the direction of the patrón's residence. "Who?" he murmured to himself. "Who would do it, and from there?"

Esteven raised a thick arm and pointed in the direction of the cemetery. "A good, clean, straight shot. Much closer, amigo. He would still have to be a good marksman, but it could be done more easily from the house."

"Juan, someone would have seen him."

Esteven slowly shook his head, looking steadily at Dr. Brunner, eyes narrowed again. "No. The day of el patrón's funeral everyone was out there, even the little children and the old grandmothers. Everyone from the big house, everyone from all the other houses. Amigo, if he had been a thief he could have robbed every house around the yard and ridden away without being seen." The intense, narrowed gaze remained fixed on George Brunner. "If he fired from the patio . . . There are walls on three sides. Even if the yard had not been empty, no one would have been able to see him. Or from inside the house, on the west side. You see?"

George saw. But it took a while for the incredulity to pass. He had been baffled by the lack of tracks, but it had never occurred to him that the knoll had not been the rifleman's point of vantage. The lack of tracks had been what had brought him out here, and now it seemed there had been no tracks because no one had been atop the knoll to make them.

He turned. "Juan, is there any way to prove that he really was in the big house, or somewhere else in the yard?"

"No. How? By tracks? Look out there. The dust has imprints of a hundred sets of tracks going and coming. It is always like that."

"Any other way? Were strangers seen on the range. Did any strangers ride in looking for work or to water a horse, or for any reason?"

"No. I would have heard if a stranger had been out yonder or in the yard. Amigo, I lie awake at night. . . . He had to have been in the big house, or the patio maybe, or he could have been in the barn. There are many places he could hide while waiting to get his killing shot. But it was not at the hill, and I have no idea who he was. I can think of reasons why he would want to kill our lady. Well, *maybe* why he would want to. So can you, but what good does that do? He is unknown to any of us. He was not even seen." Esteven flapped his arms and looked toward the shoeing shed, where the young vaqueros were talking loudly. He got to his feet and faced George Brunner. "This must be a secret," he said. "Do you know why? Because he did not kill her, and if we have no

39

idea who he was and he finds out you and I are interested, the next time his marksmanship will make my wife a widow and your friends in town pallbearers. Yes?"

While George lingered on the old bench watching the burly overseer walk away, it crossed his mind that it would not only be he himself and the mayordomo who might become targets; by now the bushwhacker certainly knew Maria Teresa was still alive.

He went after the big long-faced livery horse and struck out on the trail to town. The heat was overpowering; there was nothing he could do about it, and without appreciable shade he was damp all over by the time he meandered down an alley to the rear of the livery barn.

After leaving the horse he crossed to the east side of the road, where shadows were deepest, and went up to the saloon. He was thirsty. Beer in saloons on the South Desert was usually tepid, but ingenious barmen had their own way of counteracting this on hot days; they put a small piece of peppermint beside each glass. The illusion was of a cold drink, whether it was cold or not.

It was a little early for the evening trade but the saloon had about a dozen patrons, counting a poker session in a far, cool corner, the six players sending pale clouds of bluish smoke upward.

When the barman brought George Brunner's beer and piece of peppermint, he cocked an eye and said, "Old Doc was lookin' for you. Seems some woman over in Mex Town was having a hard time of it."

"Baby?" George asked, raising his glass.

"Yeah. He made out all right, but he was sure red in the face when he come by here an hour or so back."

George nodded and sipped his beer, looking around when a lanky, pale-eyed man in faded shirt and britches eased in beside him and smiled. He flexed his left hand. "No pain," he said.

George remembered him from earlier. Barnard. Something-or-other Barnard. He smiled back. "I'm glad. Are you keeping it clean?"

The tall man settled forward to lean on the bar and order a drink. "Can't always do that, but I try."

"Any redness yet? Any fever in the arm, any swelling or bluish color?"

"Nope. I think you did it up right, Doctor."

George looked at the sun-bronzed man and decided to break one of Homer Hudspeth's rules. He said, "I came down here from Nebraska, too."

The lanky man continued to lean on the bar. When the barman came along he nodded for a refill of his beer glass. Then he looked around slowly. "You ever been in Missouri?" he asked.

George shook his head. "Never have."

"That's where I was longest. Missouri, and once in a while over into Kansas."

"Good cattle country?"

Barnard accepted his refill from the barman before replying. "No. Kansas is as flat as the top of this bar. When the summer sun arrives it bakes everything in sight. Missouri is better. It gets plenty of summer rain, and it's not so flat. Lots of timber and good bottomland. But it's a mite crowded for cattle. I started out riding for an old Confederate who was a free-grazer. Tough old cuss. But he upped and died, so I come west."

"By way of Nebraska?"

"Yeah. Now I'm down where in another forty miles a man can fry eggs on a rock almost any day of the year, eh?"

George smiled. "I guess so. I've never been more than ten miles from Lordsville, but I've heard stories of how quick the good land plays out and the real desert takes hold."

Barnard shifted a little but remained in his place. "Hard to find work down here. Most of the riders been on the same ranches all their lives, and their pappies before them. I never saw country like this before."

George had to agree with that. "Me either. I've been here two years now and I still get surprised every week."

Barnard flexed his left hand again, then drained his glass and sat up. "You expect this bandage ought to be changed tomorrow, maybe?"

George was sure of it. "Yes. If you get there early, about breakfast time. I've got to leave town later."

Barnard nodded. "I'll be there."

George watched Barnard's loose-jointed, rangy reflection in the backbar mirror as the man left the saloon, and it suddenly occurred to him that he had forgotten all about riding toward that knoll to see if he would hear Juan Esteven beating an anvil. Hell!

CHAPTER 4

GOD AND
CARBOLIC ACID

Homer Hudspeth had taken a bath. His hair stood in spiky disarray when he turned from the stove in the kitchen to nod at George as he walked in.

They got along well, always had. George said almost nothing about things he disapproved of, and Homer was an amiable old man. But this time Homer mentioned the breech delivery over in Mex Town. The way he said it made it clear that he wanted to know where his associate had been when he should have been in town.

George replied that he had taken a long horseback ride, which was the truth. But he neglected to say where the ride had taken him, and evidently Homer did not really care. He was no longer exasperated that his younger associate had not been available to help with the difficult birthing, he was simply annoyed.

George washed and took over cooking their evening meal. Homer relinquished the chore without protest. He loathed cooking, perhaps because after all these years he could still not manage it.

After supper Homer retired early. For him it had been a strenuous day. Forty years earlier the same kind of a day would have left him with plenty of vigor. Forty years was a long time, and it made a difference.

George went out to the rear garden, which still had scraggly vestiges of flowers Homer had planted years earlier. They were uncared for now; weeds had largely taken over. Neglect, particularly during the hot season when water was too precious to waste on flowers, had taken its toll.

Still, it was a quiet place, hidden from the main roadway by the house, the only public thoroughfare a dusty and little-used alley. Here, with soft evening settling gently, George sat on a dilapidated bench to recapitulate the events of the day and to speculate on their significance.

On the ride over to Lord's Land he had been curious about the shooting of Maria Antonia, which still troubled him. But on the ride back, and now while sitting relaxed in the cooling evening, he was almost as curious about how the shooting had been accomplished as by whom, and for what purpose.

As Juan Esteven had said, it was not difficult to imagine why someone had wanted Maria Antonia dead. Lord's ranch was vast and very profitable; a lot of people probably coveted Lord's Land.

The difficulty for George Brunner was trying to imagine who wanted it badly enough to kill the last of the Lord family to get it. In his two years of residency in the area he had met most of the people at one time or another, and that included other landholders. He thought of them individually and at some length. While some, many of them in fact, had impressed him as being capable of violence, all could be eliminated one after another, for different reasons. He ended up exactly where he had started; there was nothing sufficently tangible to warrant fixed suspicion.

He yawned, gazing around the yard, and laughed at himself. He was a physician, not a detective. But he also happened to be an individual of insatiable curiosity. He went inside and got ready for bed. As he lay in bed, he rationalized that a physician was also a detective; he had to be, because physicians could only successfully treat ailments when they had diagnosed them as a result of investigating the symptoms.

His mind drifted until it settled on a different, more fascinating subject, and he was still dwelling on it when he went to sleep: Maria Antonia Lord.

In the morning, while he and Homer were having breakfast, Barnard arrived. George left Homer at the kitchen table and took the day's first patient to a small examination room, where the smell of carbolic acid was very strong.

They said very little while George removed the bandage and studied the injury with meticulous attention. He went after a basin of hot water to cleanse it. There was no sign of infection but as George told the rangeman, while this was certainly a cause for relief it was not a guarantee. He worked carefully over the injury. The swelling was gone, the process of healing was progressing, there was reason to be hopeful. But George said nothing of this to the rangeman, even when he asked.

The man's blue eyes were fixed on George as he was bandaging the wound. "I met a Mex lady yesterday over the east side of Main Street," he said. "She took me to see her aunt. The old lady is one of their healers."

George's gaze rose to the taller man's face. "A *curandera?*"

The rangy man nodded. "I couldn't remember it, but that's the word. It means she —"

"I know what it means," George said brusquely. "And what did she tell you?"

"Well, Doctor, her notion was for me to take off the bandage while she made up a pot of mud and herbs. She wanted me to let her slather her medicine over the wound and then sit somewhere until it dried hard. Then, she said, she would peel it off in chunks, and the bad thing that lived in my arm would be pulled out, too."

George said nothing as he looked steadily at the other man.

Barnard remained impassive as long as he could, then he laughed. "Doctor, you don't look like this kind of treatment is one of your favorites."

George, who was usually restrained in matters such as this, replied with no restraint at all. "Pure hogwash, Mr. Barnard. Absolutely useless — and in fact, it probably would have caused your arm to become infected."

The rangeman's eyes twinkled. "It ain't Mr. Barnard, it's Walt Barnard, and I only went down there because this real pretty Mex lady I met wanted me to. Doctor, when I was a kid back in Missouri there was folks around the countryside that used herbs and certain kinds of tree bark and suchlike for medicines. But anyone knew better'n to put mud on an open wound."

George eyed the lanky man with a dawning suspicion that Walt Barnard had done this deliberately, to get a reaction. He had gotten it. George began cleaning up the examination room table. It was early in the day for teasing. He had not even finished his breakfast. "Mr. Barnard," he began.

"Walt. Just plain Walt."

"Walt, yesterday you told me it was a strange country. I'd say you encountered one of its unique characteristics. I wouldn't defend one of those old women, but I will tell you this: These people have been cut off from the rest of the world for a very long time, so they've had to grope for many substitutes. Curanderas are one of them. Dr. Hudspeth has had to battle them, as well as ignorance and superstition, a long time. He told me once that judging from the slow rate of progress he's made, the territory will probably be another hundred and fifty years learning about such simple things as hygiene, let alone proper and proven medical practices."

Barnard nodded in agreement, rolling down

49

his sleeve. "Not just down here, Doctor," he said, buttoning the cuff. "Back where I come from, too. Only back there they've done a little better. Tell me something. I'd judge from the looks of you that you ain't been a doctor for long. Why down here? Why not up in Denver or over at Omaha? There's plenty of ignorance and poor judgment to go around, but in those places they've come ahead."

George had finished cleaning up. He leaned against a dark oak cabinet with wavy glass doors, which held Homer Hudspeth's surgical instruments. "I wanted a challenge, Walt. I was full of ideals. The world was waiting for my skills."

Barnard had finished with his cuff and was now standing relaxed, eyeing the shorter man. In a voice as dry as corn husks he said, "Yeah. The knight on the white horse. I'm older'n you, so I can tell you. Life takes its own sweet time turning them ideas to plain old dust, a little at a time." Walt Barnard gave George a death's-head smile. "Only that's not exactly what I meant by askin' why you're down here, one or two day's ride from the Mex border. That lady I met yesterday told me this country is what the Mexicans call a 'funnel.' Just about everyone you see here today ain't here tomorrow. It's a funnel for folks who are heading toward the border an' across it from up north — for their own safety."

As they stood looking at each other George had a dawning idea: Walter Barnard thought he, George Brunner, was down here because he wanted to lose himself, because somewhere along George's back trail there was a bad experience, a violated ethic or even a serious crime.

George smiled faintly and shook his head. "No. I simply had to start enlightening mankind somewhere, and when this opportunity arrived, I took it. Anyway, I'd never heard anything but romantic tales of the South Desert country."

Barnard's pale blue eyes did not leave George's face, but the corners of his wide mouth drooped. "Sure," he said, reaching for his hat. "Well, I got to go look after my horse. How much this time — four bits?"

George nodded and watched Barnard dig in a pocket for the silver coin, which he placed on the examination table. He was turning toward the door when George stopped him. "Walt," he said earnestly, "that's the gospel truth."

The unconvinced rangeman faced around with his hand on the door latch. "In this godforsaken place?" He made it sound as though only an idiot or a simpleton would be that naïve.

After Barnard was gone George returned to the kitchen to finish his breakfast. He was not very talkative, so Homer busied himself at the dishpan. Only after George had finished his second cup of coffee as the sun was climbing did Homer say, "If you're going to make the call at the Lord place, you'd better stir your stumps. It's going to be another hot one today."

George was within sight of the sprawling ranch yard when morning coolness yielded to the heat that Homer had predicted.

He handed his horse to the *remudero* out front of the barn, and the man's broad smile offered a silent welcome. George untied his satchel from behind the cantle and went through dust to the patio gateway, and from there to the steel-reinforced front door. He rapped on it.

This time is was Doña Teresa Maria who opened the door, her vinegary expression unchanged and unchanging as she wordlessly moved aside. In a sepulchral voice she said, "She did not rest well last night."

George stopped to search the forbidding face. "Bleeding?"

"No. No bleeding, but I think she is feverish." Doña Teresa Maria led the way, moving erectly and soundlessly. At the bedroom door she turned. "I think it was yesterday that you upset her."

As they entered, the marble white face on a thin pillow showed its very black eyes unblinkingly fixed on them. George crossed over, placed his satchel on the small marble-topped table, and with his heavy gold watch in one hand felt for the pulse of Maria Antonia with his other. The only sound was distant and muted; outside men were shouting encouragement to a vaquero saddling a green colt.

George placed the cool wrist back on Maria Antonia's stomach, pocketed the watch, and smiled into the midnight eyes. "Very good. Now tell me, how did you sleep last night?"

The black eyes flicked to Tiá Theresa Maria and back. "The room was very warm last night. I wanted most of the blankets turned back."

George accepted that. Such a simple explanation to the anxiety he had felt since entering the room. It had been very warm in Lordsville last night too.

He leaned over her. "I want you to take a very slow breath. Stop inhaling the instant there is pain." He watched closely. When the intake of breath stopped and the air was exhaled, he straightened up. Improvement. He smiled again, shot Teresa Maria a look, and pulled a chair around beside the bed and sat down. "We will not change the bandages. No, no, don't turn on your side. I want to explain something to you."

Maria Antonia settled back weakly. She had not said a word and she still did not.

"I think you should know," he continued, "that lung shots almost invariably collapse the lung. If it is only one lung, that is bad enough, but a person can still breathe. If it collapses both lungs the person dies." He smiled at the beautiful woman. "Rarely is a lung not collapsed by a bullet wound. Very rarely."

"And one of mine is collapsed?" the beautiful woman said faintly.

George continued to smile at her. "That is what I wanted to explain to you. No, it did not collapse, and this is the first time since I've been treating people I've ever encountered such a thing. It not only has not collapsed, but I am certain repair to the damage is in progress inside your body. Recovery is going to be slow and lengthy, but what I would not have told you even yesterday I will tell you now: You will recover."

Tiá Teresa Maria breathed softly. "It is a miracle." She made the sign of the cross. "Maria, it is the will of God."

Maria Antonia looked upward at her aunt.

Her eyes were becoming misty, and the tight-pressed lips loosened. George watched her transition with fascination. The iron will of the Lords, which never accepted the nearness of death, was now being replaced by the emotions of a woman.

He arose and went to the small barred rear window and stood there as the women touched, the older one crying very softly and gently.

George's window was recessed deeply in the massive adobe wall. It had artistic wrought iron, in scrolls, set in the adobe. It appeared to be an example of some ranch artisan's simple genius, but in fact its purpose was more prosaic: to prevent the wraithlike Indians, whose war against the newcomers in their land had lasted over two hundred years, from getting inside to cut throats in the small dark hours of the night. Such things had occurred many times before the protective ironwork had been devised and installed, and it had even happened a few times afterward.

He returned to the marble-topped table to close and buckle his satchel, watching the weeping women briefly before he let himself out of the room and down through the house to the front door. Beyond, there were nesting birds in the patio's ancient trees. Here shade made fragrant by well-tended beds of flowers left him feeling that to shoot someone from this serene and lovely place was a form of blasphemy.

He went to the west wall and found a place where decades of sudden desert storms had worn the adobe down, where he stood looking in the direction of the ranch graveyard. His idea that a man with a long-barreled rifle could have performed his act of attempted murder from this spot was confirmed, if the man was a marksman — and of course he had been. George could even see a mound where the former master of Lord's Land was at rest.

Doña Teresa Maria came from the house, and George turned at the sound of the massive old door being opened and closed. The tall, almost gaunt woman stood in shade, looking at him. "You have made up for yesterday," she told him, in what he assumed was forgiveness.

He smiled at her. "If you knew how many times I can't bring that kind of news to people, you would understand how I feel when I can. Nevertheless, she must not move. She must not even breathe deeply. Now comes the hardest part, Doña Teresa. She must fight her impatience just as hard as she fought the other thing. Even harder, I think. If you watched over her before, you will have to be even more watchful now."

The tall woman's slightly hawkish features wore an expression of uncharacteristic serenity. "I will take care of her. I will see that she does not move. God has spared her, Doctor. I will tell the mayordomo to organize a period of thanks. God has smiled. I'll send for Father O'Malley. This miracle has been God's work."

George smiled, shifting uncomfortably, bowed slightly, and walked out into the yard, where sun and dust and a turquoise sky as flawless as only desert skies can be spanned the horizon.

Later, as he was mounting up after securing the satchel behind his cantle, he squinted in the direction of the hacienda and said, "God and carbolic acid, Aunt Teresa."

CHAPTER 5

AN EMERGENCY

He reached Lordsville with the sun off-center on its westerning glide, and before he handed his reins to the liveryman he was told that Dr. Hudspeth had been called to the old mission, which lay a short distance from town, for an emergency.

The liveryman who told him this had clearly looked forward to being able to hold the younger doctor's undivided attention. He did not avoid milking his moment of importance to the last drop. He loosened the latigo slowly and in silence. While looping it through the cinch ring he said, "It's Father O'Malley. Somethin' happened." He raised the saddle, slung it over his arm, and started for the dingy, smelly little harness room, George following. After draping the saddle by a stirrup from a wooden peg, the liveryman said, "Old Doc was red as a beet when he went hustlin' past an hour or so back. He called to me to tell you to come out there as soon as you come back."

George did not thank the liveryman. He left the barn clutching his satchel. Reaching the dilapidated old mission, which had once been a jewel in the crown of missions that had been established, two days apart by mule, from Chihuahua to upper New Mexico Territory, required a very brisk walk of about two thirds of a mile. Ordinarily he would have been conscious of the heat; this time he was not.

Originally there had been a handsome gilded cross atop the mission's red-tiled high roof. It had disappeared a century earlier. Its replacement was a simple wooden creation held together by green rawhide. It listed to one side.

The mission was still surrounded by an extensive mud wall, which had been greviously eroded by rain in places. Inside there was a large burial area, a number of sheds, and some large corrals for much larger and stronger animals than were now driven inside them every night — goats for milk and meat.

Along the rear of the mission there was a long, broad, red-tiled walkway, which was always cool, thanks to the ingenuity and foresight of the builders, who had shaded it with a sloping overhang, solidly boarded on top to keep out the sun's rays.

George knew O'Malley and his mission. He had sat on a number of hot evenings on that rear loggia drinking red wine and enjoying the priest's company and conversation. This afternoon as he hurried down the long cool corridor, his boots sending echoes upward from the old red tiles, he was intercepted midway by a dark youth who appeared like a shadow from one of the many identical doors. George slackened his pace as the youth waved him toward the open door.

The small room was meagerly furnished. Light came from three candles on a wooden shelf that held old worn leather-bound books. There was a low dresser with a chipped white washbasin on it. Beside the dresser was a wooden closet, crudely fashioned, with leather hinges to both its long narrow doors.

This room, like every other room of the old mission, smelled very faintly but unmistakably of cedarwood incense. For two centuries at least, cedar smoke had risen slowly somewhere in the large building at least once a day, and more often on traditional holy days.

The bed was along the west wall. It was a simple four-poster with a low footboard and a modest headboard. The mattress rustled every time the man lying on it moved even slightly. It had been stuffed with dry corn husks. Beneath the mattress were latticed lengths of maguey rope to serve as bedsprings.

When George appeared in the doorway, Doctor Hudspeth got to his feet from a small low stool, and taking George's arm, led him back out to the long concourse. Looking over his shoulder, he said, "Stroke. He can't move his right arm. I think there is damage to his right leg too. I'd better go back for some medicine. You talk to him, George." Homer gave George's arm a slight squeeze, then went briskly back the way he had come. George watched for a moment before returning to the poorly lit little room. He sank down upon the low stool Homer had vacated, and Father O'Malley smiled at him. George did not smile back. He took the inert right arm in his hands and pinched. Neither of them spoke. Father O'Malley gently shook his head.

George looked around for the Mexican youth. When their eyes met he said, "Is there whiskey?" The youth shrugged and looked inquiringly toward the bed. Father O'Malley pointed with his jaw and said, "In the kitchen, behind the sack of potatoes in a corner. Sandoval, two of the tin cups."

George had been listening. He looked steadily at Father O'Malley. There had been no slurring or thickness of speech. He stood up and went to the priest, leaning down to find a heartbeat. He did that twice, then he straightened up, looking puzzled. "How did it happen?" he asked.

The priest's large-boned body was inert, his two hundred well-distributed pounds were flaccid. "I was coming to my room," said Father O'Malley, "from the chapel. I had climbed to the old bell tower. Of course, the bells have been gone a long time, many years, but it is such a fine view from up there. It is a place for private prayer."

"Father, you shouldn't have —"

"Yes. Well, I had been up there, and after climbing down I walked over here. I was short of breath. That is quite a climb. So I sat on the piñon bench a few yards north of my room. I had been sitting there to catch my breath for about five minutes."

"And . . . ?"

The priest looked at George's faintly puzzled frown. "It began as a slight burning sensation. Then it moved gradually to my right leg and right arm."

"And your chest hurt?"

Father O'Malley shook his head. "No. Just

my right leg and arm."

"Your head?"

"No, George. My right leg and arm."

George turned as the youth returned with two tin cups and an earthenware jug. He took them, thanked the youth, and poured whiskey into one cup, which he asked the priest to hold in his left hand. When this was done George put his arms under Father O'Malley's shoulders and strained to raise him so he could swallow. Then he lowered him and put the cup aside.

He smiled. "Father, where were you born?" O'Malley answered matter-of-factly. "And tell me the names of your parents, your brothers and sisters, your aunts and uncles."

O'Malley reeled off names one after another, his eyes fixed on Dr. Brunner's face. When he had finished he said, "It proves my mind and memory were not affected, George?"

George dropped back down onto the little three-legged stool. "It proves you didn't have a stroke, Father." After a moment of watching immense relief come over the older man's face, George rose, took one of the candles, and went back outside, where shadows were thickening by the minute, jerking his head for the youth to come with him.

He led the way to the very old handmade

piñon-wood bench and stood looking at it for a moment before signaling for the youth to hold the candle lower. There was nothing on the bench, but beneath it, where it had fallen in its death struggles, was a half grown scaly-backed scorpion. George touched it with his toe. It was not dead yet; the menacing tail swung high above the creature's back, poised for the thrust.

George stood up and killed the scorpion with his boot. He looked at the Mexican youth, whose eyes were perfectly round.

They returned to the priest's room. He was sound asleep. George thanked the youth for his vigil and told him he would no longer be needed. After the boy left, George went back out to the loggia to lean against the hand-textured mud wall.

Homer arrived a half hour later. He was carrying a large leather satchel. When he made out George's silhouette in the fragrant dusk he veered over and whispered, "Is he gone?" Homer's breath was powerful.

George shook his head. "No, he's sleeping."

Homer sank down upon a bench ten yards south of the lethal one, placed the satchel between his feet, and fished for a blue bandana to wipe away his sweat. "In time he can most likely do his work. I don't suppose crippled priests are unheard of, are they?"

George didn't think so. "No. But he didn't have a stroke, Homer."

The older man started so suddenly he nearly upset the satchel. He didn't open his mouth, he just stared. George sank down on his haunches beside the bench and explained about the scorpion. "He sat on it, it stung him, probably several times. It was still alive when I found it beneath the bench."

Homer was sputtering. "But the *symptoms*, George."

"Well yes, except that he could move his fingers and toes and his voice was absolutely normal, and so was his memory." George looked up at the older man. "It would be natural to believe it was a stroke, Homer."

Dr. Hudspeth struggled to his feet. "Are you sure?"

"Yes. Go in there and awaken him. Roll him over and take down his britches. The scorpion either stung him on the behind or the back of his legs, but the inflamed punctures should be visible even by candlelight."

Hudspeth craned around toward the open door, where the weak light was barely able to reach. "No," he said, and shook his head. "There's no need to wake him. I'll come back in the morning."

George tiptoed back inside for his satchel.

Father O'Malley's shadowed eyes were open, watching him. After explaining about the scorpion, George smiled. "Drink the rest of that cup of whiskey and get a lot of sleep. It takes a while for the poison to work through your system. I'd guess that by tomorrow afternoon you'll feel much better. In another two or three days you'll be back doing your chores."

Homer was waiting in semidarkness, and as they started back down the long walkway, Homer clutching his large satchel, he said, "It just seemed so natural, like hundreds of patients I've seen who've had light strokes."

George said nothing until they were back on the plank walk in town. Then he smiled at the older man, whose expression appeared as a mixture of chagrin and embarrassment. "That's the second scorpion sting I've treated down here, Homer. The only reason I doubted it was a stroke was that the first bite victim was sixteen years old. Too young for a stroke. This time everything was the same. It looked like a stroke, except for the moving fingers, the perfectly normal tone of voice, and the alert way he responded to questions."

Homer led the way into the house, shaking his head. He put the big satchel aside and headed straight for the kitchen. George followed and lit the coal-oil lamp while Homer rummaged in his special cupboard. By the time George had the woodstove fired up and the coffeepot on a rear burner, Homer had swallowed several jolts of whiskey. It appeared to ameliorate his anxiety. He grunted and shifted around in the chair to look at George, standing by the stove. "The symptoms were right," he said. "Anyway, it was dark in his room."

George nodded in agreement and took down only one cup. He did not believe Homer would care for coffee, and he was right.

They sat in the kitchen for an hour, talking and relaxing. It had been a long day for them both. When Homer neglected to ask about Maria Antonia Lord, George told him of his visit, of her improvement, and asked Homer what he knew about the Gallegos woman. It appeared that Homer knew quite a bit. He probably knew quite a bit about everyone in what he considered his territory. But what he said about Tía Teresa Maria was no more than George could have guessed. She was a widow. Her husband had ranched – not on the scale of David Lord, but close to it. After his death she had become a recluse. Her retainers ran the ranch. She spent a great deal of time praying. There was a small private chapel on the Meir ranch. Teresa Maria had been considered the most beautiful woman between Chihuahua and

Albuquerque at one time. Her marriage had been childless. She was a woman of iron will. She was the sister of Maria Antonia Lord's mother.

Homer finished, mopped his eyes, left half the handkerchief hanging from a coat pocket, and got to his feet with an effort. Leaning heavily on the tabletop, he said he thought he would retire.

After his departure George refilled his cup, turned down the stove damper, and sat for a while, sipping coffee and thinking.

Dogs barked over on the east side of town and northward — nocturnal creatures crept into town after nightfall to rummage in refuse barrels. George rinsed his cup in the dishwater bucket and went off to his room.

There was a majestic full moon tonight. Its light was pure and faintly silvery where it came into the room. On these full-moon nights, so he had been told, a secret sect call Penitentes convened far out and scourged one another and themselves as they struggled to carry a large wooden cross in a ritual ceremony notable for the groans and bloodshed that marked their passage. The scourging was done with chains.

CHAPTER 6

THE DISCOVERY

Homer was sleeping when George went out to the kitchen. He did not awaken him. He had never awakened him when Homer overslept. He fired up the stove to take the chill off and went down to the café for breakfast.

All the early morning diners were men, and all of them were local workers such as the blacksmith's helper, the old man who served as clerk in the general store, and Marshal Kandelin. Breakfast at the Lordsville café was a convocation of men who knew one another well. The result was teasing, good-natured insults, raw jokes passed up and down the counter, and gossip. George was welcomed with questions. Father O'Malley's sudden ailment was a matter of lively interest, not that he had any parishioners at the café but because he was liked.

George said Father O'Malley had sat on a scorpion and the noise of laughter reached to the far side of the roadway. When Frank Kandelin laughed George noticed his two gold eyeteeth. They only showed when the town marshal threw back his head and roared with laughter.

After breakfast Kandelin caught George crossing the road and invited him to the jailhouse for a cup of freshly brewed coffee, something those who dined at the café only got on Saturdays, which was when the café man emptied out his reused grounds and made a fresh batch for the next week.

Marshal Kandelin was in an expansive mood; George's information concerning the priest's ailment seemed to have added to it. With his small gray eyes showing amusement, Marshal Kandelin went to the stove to draw off two cups, saying, "I saw Homer go out there late yesterday like his shirttail was on fire." Kandelin brought one cup to George and went to sit behind his table with the other.

George looked at the lawman, raising his cup — then his hand froze in midair. Atop a litter of papers directly in front of Frank Kandelin was a wanted dodger. The picture on it was of the man George had been treating. Walt

Barnard. George tried to read the smaller print upside down and failed, but he had little difficulty reading the large black boldface print. Walter Barnard was wanted for three murders in Nebraska. The bounty was five hundred dollars.

Marshal Kandelin interrupted George's thoughts with a question. "How's the lady doin' out at the Lord place?"

George sipped and set the cup down before replying. "Better than anyone had a right to expect, Marshal."

Kandelin's little gray eyes were speculative. "You expect her to recover?"

George nodded. "I'd guess she has about an eighty percent chance of recovering, but it'll take a long time."

Kandelin tasted his coffee and put the cup aside. George watched him briefly, then said, "They told me you went out there, Marshal."

Kandelin leaned back in his chair. "Yeah." He looked straight at George Brunner. "The mayordomo was out with some of the riders, but a couple of fellers took me out to that knoll where they said the bushwhacker fired from."

"Did you find anything?"

"Some tracks. But right after the shootin' I guess half the riders on the place went out there. One set of marks looks pretty much like another set if all the horses are shod with flat plates. What I wanted to find was a shell casing, maybe some cigarette butts, anything that would prove he'd really been up there, because George, that is one hell of a distance from the graveyard. He'd have had to been carryin' a long-barreled rifle, and he should have had a spyglass or something to pick her out at that distance."

George drank half his coffee and set the cup on a wall-bench. "Anything else turn up, Marshal?"

"No. An' I doubt that it will." As he said this, Kandelin rocked forward and planted both thick arms on the littered table that served as his desk. "Those Mexicans close up like a clam when they see a badge. I know; I've been around them a lot of years. She's got a hell of a lot of them out there. That's one of those old-time ranches where the vaqueros got families livin' with 'em." Kandelin's little eyes narrowed. "Those old-time places aren't so much cattle ranches as they are settlements. Sometimes the Mexes been livin' an' workin' on those places for up to three generations. George, findin' someone who will tell you anything among all those people is about as easy as bear rassling."

Brunner leaned forward, as if to rise. "No suspects then?"

Kandelin stood. "I don't know as I'd go that far," he said, and rapped the wanted poster face up in front of him. "I just got this dodger. I keep thinkin' I've seen this man." Kandelin handed George the poster. "I got to ask around town."

George read all the small print and handed the poster back. "Three killings," he murmured as he rose.

Kandelin nodded, studying the dodger. "Hired killer. It don't say so here but that's what he is, as sure as I'm standin' here. I've read a hundred of these things, maybe two hundred, and the hired killers always got about the same things written about them."

George reached the door, then turned. "You think he might have shot Maria Lord?"

Frank Kandelin was unprepared to go quite that far. "Well, he's down here. Sure as hell I've seen him. An' maybe he come here to do a little job, an' maybe he's just another one heading for the border. When I nail him I'll know more." Kandelin let the dodger slip from his fingers to the desktop. "Either way, he's worth five hundred dollars dead or alive." Kandelin was smiling. George nodded and went back out into the sun-bright, refreshingly cool morning.

On his walk northward to the Hudspeth house he was puzzled by the name on the

73

poster. It was the same name Walt Barnard had given him. Either the man was a fool or he was confident he was too far from Nebraska to be caught by the law — otherwise he certainly would not use his natural name. Of one thing George felt certain; Walt Barnard was no fool.

Homer was eating breakfast when George walked into the kitchen. Homer did not look good. That he had a hangover was obvious, but it was more than that.

George half filled a cup of coffee and took it to the table with him. Homer nodded, averting wet eyes as he began to mumble. "I should have stripped him," he said, spearing fried beef as black as boot leather. "But it was a classical case of stroke, George."

Brunner smiled. "Hell, Homer, how many diagnoses have you made? Ten thousand in fifty years? I've only been at the trade four years and I can recall being wrong more often than I think you've ever been."

It was not the truth, but it had the desired effect. Homer raised his eyes and smiled. George refilled his coffee cup and asked, "Has that rangeman with the nail gash been around yesterday or today?"

Homer chewed and swallowed before replying. "Not that I know of. They lose the swelling and they think they're fit as a fiddle, so they don't return. Most of them who look like that man looked can't stand leaving four bits with us every day or two." Homer finished his boot-sole steak and half black fried potatoes and shoved the plate away as he pulled his coffee cup closer. "Are you going out to the Lord place today?" he asked.

George had not thought about it. He might have, in time, if he hadn't been shocked down to his heels by what he had seen on Marshal Kandelin's table. "I don't know. I didn't change the dressings yesterday, so maybe I ought to. Why? You have something in mind?"

"No. I've got to look in on that Mex woman who had the baby, and there's an old man over there I should look at, too. Nothing critical. I've been working on him for ten years, when I get the time."

"What's wrong with him?"

Homer smiled. "Same thing that's wrong with me – old. Just plain old." He laughed and struggled up from the chair to go after more coffee, asking if George needed a refill and receiving a negative answer. It was not even ten o'clock yet, and George had already had five cups of the stuff. What made that unique was the fact that George did not really care much for coffee, but he lived in an age when people used almost any excuse to drink it.

75

He waited until Homer was seated again before asking if he intended to go out to the mission. Homer looked into his cup while replying. "I suppose so. I know right now when I go out there O'Malley's going to look at me like I'm a doddering old fool who ought to quite the medical trade."

George rose and said he thought he'd go down and look in on his horse. He did not have a family, but he had a good strong sorrel gelding being boarded at the livery barn, and he was fond of the animal. So fond of him in fact that if the weather was really bad, or if he had to ride a great distance, he hired a livery horse so his sorrel would not be put through hardship.

Homer raised disapproving eyes. "You're going to end up with a fat animal that's as soft as punk unless you exercise him. It's all well and good to make a pet of a saddle animal, George, but you overdo it. If you ever have to ride him hard, he's going to drop dead under you."

George had heard almost the identical words from the liveryman. He left the house, his hat tipped down in front to shade eyes that had learned to crinkle from reflected sunlight. Across the road Marshal Kandelin was standing in front of the saloon in serious conversation with the proprietor. George would have bet new money he knew what they were talking about — the man from Nebraska.

As usual, Lordsville was busy this morning. By afternoon, when the heat arrived, it would be possible to shoot a cannon down through town without even hitting a dog, let alone two-legged creatures.

The proprietor was not around when George reached the gloomy runway, but that mean-looking hostler was. He told George where his sorrel was, leaning on a manure fork and wagging his head as George went down to the stall and began talking to his horse. The hostler hoisted his fork and went out back. In an old unused corral across the alley there were two huge manure piles. Local people helped themselves for flower beds and vegetable gardens, but there was one thing about dunging out horse barns — the piles continued to grow after gardeners no longer needed fertilizer. This time of year the blue tail flies rose in swarms when anyone approached. The hostler lingered in shade, looking over there. He was a thin, tall man with a shock of graying brown hair and a pursed, sour-appearing mouth.

He had intended to go over there and work the piles, but a rider coming down the alley from the north distracted him; he was perfectly willing to be distracted, so he leaned on the fork watching the horseman. When he was close the hostler straightened up and moved aside for the horseman to ride on in. But he dismounted outside and led his rawboned big bay horse up the runway.

George heard the horse and turned at about the same time the rider saw him. George froze, but the lanky horseman smiled and said, "Goin' to be another hot one, Doctor," and took his animal to the tierack to be offsaddled.

The hostler ambled up to take the saddle, blanket, and bridle to the harness room. He returned in a few minutes to untie the bay horse and lead it away. The bay's owner shoved back his hat and strolled over to where George was standing. He leaned on the half door, looking in, and in that easy way he had of speaking, he said, "Your animal?"

George glanced furtively up in the direction of the roadway. "Yes," he replied.

"Good horse, Doctor. Too fat and soft, but that's not his fault, is it?"

Their eyes met. The lanky man was still smiling. George asked how his arm was and he held forth his hand as he flexed the fingers. "Fine. Healing good, and the swelling is gone."

George turned back to look in at his horse as he quietly said, "Nebraska isn't far enough, Walt."

Walt's smile faded. He studied the medical practitioner's profile and slowly pushed back off the half door. "Is that a fact?"

George also straightened up, but he said nothing; he simply looked Walt in the eye, nodded, and walked away, heading toward the front entrance of the barn. Outside, brilliant sunlight bounced back from storefronts and roadway dust.

He crossed over on his way to the saloon. Up there he nodded to the barman, got a glass of beer, a scrap of peppermint, and leaned against the bar in the cool big room, looking at himself in the backbar mirror.

He had already decided that Walt Barnard was not a fool. That being so, within an hour – unless George had been very incorrect in his judgment of the man – Walt would be a long way southward and still riding, heat or no heat.

The beer tasted strongly of malt, but it did wonders for a faint feeling of guilt. He had a second glass. By the time he had half finished that one his guilt was completely gone.

There was only one other customer along the bar, down where the counter made a turn to meet the east wall. After the barman had served this other customer he returned to where George was leaning and said, "Something's going on. I don't know what it is, but Frank

Kandelin nailed me out front and asked about a feller he described. Someone named Barnard."

George looked steadily at the pale, fleshy face. "Why?" he asked.

The barman spread both hands atop the counter. "He didn't say. You know how Frank is. Everything's got to be a damn mystery with him. Anyway, like I told him, men don't introduce themselves to me when they come in here. They just thump the bar and call for something to drink. As for the description, hell Doctor, it would fit two thirds of the rangemen and freighters and whatnot that come in here from time to time. But he's on some kind of a trail, sure as hell. All he'd say was that he wanted to talk to this Barnard feller."

George drained his second glass and looked uninterested. "It goes with the territory," he said. "One of the first things Homer told me when I arrived here was that Lordsville sat squarely in the middle of the outlaw trail going south to the border, and a man's best chance of living a long time down here was to see nothing, say nothing, and never ask questions."

The barman chuckled. "Homer's a wise old devil."

George agreed with that. He put two silver coins on top of the counter, and left the saloon. In the roadway someone's battered old ranch wagon was grinding dust on its way toward the stud rings set into two large trees in front of the emporium. George did not recognize either of the burnt-brown rangemen on the seat, but when they both nodded he nodded back.

Then he stepped over to the edge of the duckboards and looked southward beyond town, where the stage road ran arrow straight until heat haze blurred it into obscurity.

CHAPTER 7

DEEPENING INVOLVEMENT

George Brunner finally took all the advice he had been getting; the next morning he saddled the sorrel and struck out for the Lord place, little satchel lashed behind the cantle. It was a magnificent day, but for a change there was a spindrift of motionless cloud bank far to the northeast.

The sorrel horse watched birds break from tall grass, keeping his little ears shifting for sounds and walking with a spring in his step. He was enjoying this as much as his rider was. George talked to him. For all the difference that made he might as well have remained silent.

When they rode into the Lord yard the first vaquero they saw was Juan Esteven. He was spurred for riding but there was no horse in sight, and Juan was leaning against the front of the barn, hat tipped low, black eyes narrowed, using a straw stalk to pick his teeth.

As George was dismounting the mayordomo said, "I waited at the anvil. You rode straight toward town."

George looped his rawhide reins and smiled apologetically. "I forgot."

Juan Esteven tossed away the hay stalk and came to the hitch rack to lean on it. "It had to be something like that. I knew. You were worrying about the lady."

"How is she?" George asked, dusting both hands on his trousers.

Esteven shrugged. "*Quién sabe?* Doña Teresa Maria never leaves the house, and the girls who work there know nothing. How do you think she is?"

George glanced in the direction of the house as he replied. "Day before yesterday she looked good."

Juan Esteven leaned in thought for a moment, then bobbed his head and turned to enter the barn. George struck out for the hacienda.

Doña Teresa Maria did not open the door, it was the sturdy girl who wore bright ribbons in her hair who opened it. Without a word she led the way across the big living room and down the domed hallway to the only other door George had ever walked through in this big quiet house.

Maria Antonia was gazing out the window. When he entered she rolled her head in his direction on the low pillow, and she smiled. He tried to remember ever having seen her smile before.

He used his watch to time her pulse, then looked at her face. The color was good, the black eyes were bright. He said, "Breathe, please." She obeyed, as she had done often before. He beamed and pulled up a chair to the bedside as he said, "Very good. Tell me how you feel?"

"Much improved, Doctor. Hungry most of the time. A little restless. I wanted to talk to Juan Esteven yesterday but my aunt thought that should wait for another few days."

Her voice was soft but strong. He relaxed and draped one arm over the back of his chair. "In a few minutes we will change the bandages, but for a moment or two we can just talk."

She seemed to interpret this to mean he had more questions. She looked steadily at him without speaking.

He glanced out the barred window and back at her. "The man who shot you — did you by any chance see anything before he fired?"

84

"No. I didn't even hear the sound. But Father O'Malley, who was beside me — we were facing one another I think, when I was shot. I remember he was saying something about the responsibility being mine now, something about using it wisely. He paused and squinted past me in the direction of the yard, or that knoll. That was all I remembered until I came around in this bed. Maybe . . . I think I remember looking up at Father O'Malley after I was hit by the bullet, but I'm not sure of that. I am not certain of anything that happened after I was shot." As she finished speaking she looked intently at Dr. Brunner. "Is there someone . . . ? There is, isn't there? Does Marshal Kandelin have him?"

He shook his head and grinned. "No. The marshal has no idea who shot you. As far as I know, no one has. It is simply that I'm interested. You are sure Father O'Malley squinted when he looked behind you, as though he had seen something?"

"Yes. I am sure about what he did, but I have no idea why he did it, except that it was a very bright day. Possibly the sun hit him in the eyes as he faced me to talk."

George nodded. It hadn't been the sun. He had not been to the funeral, but he knew it had taken place close to noon, when sunlight would not strike anyone in the face — unless of course he had been lying on his back, which Father O'Malley certainly had not been doing.

He pulled his thoughts back to the present moment and rose to shed his coat and roll up his sleeves. Maria Antonia eased up onto her side without being asked to.

He had meant to ask about Tía Teresa Maria but had forgot to during their talk, so now, as he worked at examining the wounds before calling for hot water, he did ask.

The answer was brief. "She had to return home, but she promised to return this evening, or at the very latest in the morning."

He went to the door and called for a basin of water, closing the door before he knew he had been heard, except that in this silent residence with its three-feet-thick adobe exterior walls that outside sounds rarely penetrated, even a sneeze inside was heard everywhere.

When the basin arrived with a clean white towel, he went back to work. If the internal wounds were healing as well as the external ones, Maria Antonia Lord would be on her feet even sooner than George had anticipated, but he said nothing of this as he finished with the dressings and the bandages and helped the beautiful woman ease back off her side. Then he turned aside to rinse and dry his hands as she watched him.

She said, "Well, Doctor?"

He smiled at her. "Very good. Normal, healthy healing. Señorita, you have been lying here with nothing to do but think for — what is it now? About two weeks?"

She bypassed the question while looking directly at him. "And you want to know who I think did this thing."

He put the towel aside and rolled down his sleeves. "Yes."

"Doctor, I have no idea."

"Everyone has enemies."

Her brows drew inward and downward. "I have heard that. But I have no enemies who would want to murder me."

He looked wryly at her. "I have just finished looking at proof that what you said is not correct."

"But I know of no one who would shoot me. I've thought a lot about it. I could not come up with a single name, Doctor."

He shrugged into his coat and sank down onto the edge of the chair. "Señorita, not personal enemies. I can believe you have none of those — at least, none who would want to kill you. But someone else, someone who knew your father had died and you were his only heir; someone who would want your ranch.

Someone who could not buy it from you, but who might be able to gain control if you were dead."

She stared at George for a long time, expressionless and yet intent. He flapped his arms, stood up, and went to the small marble-topped table to close his satchel and reach for his hat. While his back was to her she said, "Do you know a man who owns land east of Lordsville named Carter Alvarado?"

George finished with the satchel and turned, holding it in his right hand and his hat in the other. He knew Carter Alvarado. In fact he had lanced a rattlesnake bite on his thigh a month earlier, and they had met at other times. He nodded his head. "Yes. Dr. Hudspeth cared for his wife until she died. He and Mr. Alvarado are friends."

Maria Antonia looked away and was silent for so long George thought she was not going to continue. Then she said, "He and my father got along fairly well, and my father never said anything bad about him — that I heard, anyway. But he did not like Señor Alvarado.

George studied as much of the averted face as he could see. More was coming. He guessed that Maria Antonia was having difficulty finding the right words. He was correct.

She turned slowly to meet his gaze. "He told

88

my father he wanted to marry me."

The subdued way she said this made an impression on George. He felt in his heart that many men would have wanted to marry Maria Antonia Lord. In fact, it was an idea — futile though he knew it was — that would appeal to him.

"My father told me, and Carter sent two of his vaqueros over with a beautiful palomino mare as a present."

"And you accepted it?"

"No. I sent it back. One of my distant cousins told my father Carter was furious."

George knew Alvarado fairly well. He tried to fit him into the category of a rejected lover who would want to kill the woman who had refused him, but he really did not know the man well enough to make that kind of a judgment. Homer did; he and Alvarado had been friends for years. George said, "Is that the only name you can come up with?"

Maria Antonia blushed. "Yes. You asked, Doctor."

George slapped his knees as he shot up from the chair. He left his patient looking very embarrassed. Satchel in hand he hesitated in the doorway long enough to say he would return in two days, and left the house without seeing the girl with ribbons in her hair.

Juan Esteven was still loafing in front of the barn, only now there was a saddled horse at the rack thirty feet away standing quietly beside George's sorrel. At the doctor's approach Esteven sauntered over to snug up the cinch on the sorrel and said, "How is she?"

George cleared his mind of other things before replying. "Better every day, Juan."

Esteven looked enormously relieved. He had reason to; if Maria Antonia had died lamentations would have risen from every jacal on Lord's land, and afterward the exodus would have begun.

He asked if George wanted to ride over to the knoll to test Esteven's ideas about echoes bouncing off it. George did not particularly want to — he did not believe he had to — but he nodded as he freed the sorrel, lashed his satchel, and swung into the saddle.

Juan Esteven loitered in full sunshine behind the smithy until he could see Dr. Brunner along the base of the distant hill, then hurried inside and began pounding on an anvil.

George was surprised at the fidelity of the echo. He sat looking up the slope. It looked like every other sidehill he had ever seen. He could not account for the astonishingly perfect duplication of sound. He had encountered as many echoes as other people had, but never one like this.

He turned southeast and rode around the base of the knoll, then headed directly for Lordsville. By the time he had rooftops in sight the day had worn along toward late sundown. Dusk would arrive in another hour or two, but actual darkness would be longer coming.

He left the sorrel with the sour-faced day man at the livery and went up the alley to the Hudspeth house. As he waited for Homer to arrive, he took a bath in cool water. By the time he had dressed Homer still had not arrived.

He was not particularly hungry but headed for the café anyway, taking his satchel with him because he intended to go out to the mission later. He thought Homer would be out there.

Marshal Kandelin entered the café looking glum. He and George exchanged a nod and Kandelin went and sat down at the upper end of the counter, as though he either did not want George's company or he did not want *any* company. George hoped it was the latter. He finished his meal, paid up, took the little satchel, and left the café.

On the hike out to the mission he had a little trouble getting rid of the uncomfortable feeling he'd picked up in the café. He and Frank Kandelin had never been close friends, but he could not recall ever before being avoided by the lawman.

There would be only one reason for this, and he preferred not to dwell upon it.

When he stepped up onto the tiled loggia his footsteps sent reverberating echoes far ahead. The huge old mud building was as silent as it usually was. Echoes, any kind of sound, carried far. George was midway along when a head appeared around a doorframe. Homer recognized the man walking toward him and ducked back out of sight.

George faintly and ruefully smiled to himself, satisfied that the reason Homer had not come home before sundown was because he and Father O'Malley had been sitting in cool relaxation, sampling church wine and having one of their pleasant, prolonged discussions, each of them progressing toward a splendid mellowness as the sun sank lower.

The moment he entered the room he had clear evidence in the bland faces raised to greet him that his guess had been correct.

The priest, who had twice the wine capacity of old Homer Hudspeth, was sitting on the edge of his bed. Homer was sprawled in the room's only leather-bottomed chair. Father O'Malley gestured toward a dresser on which a one-gallon earthen jug stood half empty.

George shook his head, mumbled a tactful

refusal, and went to drop down upon the low three-legged stool. For a moment the silence was awkward, then George said, "Father, the day Maria Antonia was shot, you were standing with her at the cemetery?"

Father O'Malley inclined his head, blue eyes calm.

"You turned to speak to her?"

"Yes. To explain what I was sure she already knew: that from now on she would be the patrón." O'Malley smiled softly. "I wasn't sure she didn't need someone to speak, to turn her attention briefly away from the unpleasantness out there."

George accepted this. "I understand. . . . Father, while you were talking to her, facing her, you paused and blinked or squinted your eyes because of a bright light."

The priest considered George Brunner's face for a long moment before nodding gently. "Yes. I remember that. For a second or two a dazzling reflection, almost like sunshine being bounced off a mirror, hurt my eyes. Then it was gone."

"From the top of the knoll, Father?"

"No, George, from the area of the big house, maybe from the west side of it, or maybe from near the patio wall. I did not think much about it. Things like that are likely to occur any time in a ranch yard. Someone may have polished the silver cheekpieces of his bridle, or possibly a woman had taken a mirror outside to wash and polish it."

George nodded, and finally he went over to pour a little church wine into a cracked old crockery cup.

CHAPTER 8

EL VISITADORÉ

The following morning Homer slept late again. George thought wryly that Father O'Malley probably also had. On the walk back last night George had kept something to himself he had not felt comfortable about: someone with scorpion poison in their system had no business drinking liquor in serious amounts. If Homer hadn't been half drunk himself he would have realized this.

Down at the café there were not many diners, because it was past the early morning breakfast rush. George had a wide area to himself at the counter. The old man who wore black sleeve protectors from wrist to elbow and worked at the general store was his nearest companion, and the old man, who was by nature taciturn and dour, only nodded.

95

Breakfast was almost invariably steak, potatoes, bread, and black coffee. George hardly noticed. He had reached a conclusion that was satisfactory to him: whoever had tried to kill Maria Antonia Lord had been nowhere near the knoll; he had fired from the west side of the hacienda, if he had not actually been inside, behind the patio wall. He considered mentioning this to Marshal Kandelin, and rejected the notion because of Kandelin's peculiarly antisocial behavior in the café last evening. He also speculated about that and came up with a plausible explanation. Kandelin had been working his way through town in his search for Walt Barnard yesterday. He did not find Walt, but he certainly had visited the livery barn, and if he'd shown that dodger to the bitter-faced day man, the hostler had almost certainly identified Walt as the man who had been in the barn talking to Dr. Brunner.

George returned to the roadway. The old clerk from the emporium came out behind him and put a venomous stare on George's back as he went past in the direction of the store.

There was a saddle animal drowsing at the hitch rack up in front of Homer's house, so George went up there. The horse was jet black without a white hair on him. He was young and handsome. George admired him. Of all the colors among horses, a completely black horse was one of the rarest. The horse's outfit had a big, engraved sterling horn cap. The conchos were also engraved sterling. The bridle had sterling ferrules and the cheekpieces of the bit were heavy and elaborately engraved.

George guessed Homer's visitor was one of the wealthy local ranchers and he was correct. He was the man Maria Antonia had mentioned the previous day, Don Carter Alvarado. He and Homer were in the examination room, speaking in Spanish. When George appeared in the doorway the handsome black-eyed man with pale skin nodded to him. Homer was lancing the place where Don Alvarado had been bitten by the rattlesnake. He barely more than turned his head as he reverted to English for George's sake. "An infection. Nothing to worry about."

Alvarado smiled slightly. "How is Senñorita Lord? Homer said you were looking after her."

George thought of this man's proposal of marriage and his patient's refusal of it as he answered. "Coming along surprisingly well. She is as healthy as a horse."

Alvarado's faint smile remained. "Yes. But vastly more beautiful. Her aunt is staying with her?"

George nodded. If Alvarado had not been to visit his patient, the ranchero certainly had a good source of information. But among the things George Brunner had learned about the South Desert country was that no one had secrets. As Homer had once dryly remarked, the best way to have a secret was to tell it first.

Alvarado gave a slight start and swung his attention to Dr. Hudspeth. Homer stepped back. "Disinfectant," he explained. "It's not working unless it stings a little."

The cowman's even, almost aristocratic features showed little as he leaned around to examine the fresh bandage; then he slid off the table and hoisted his trousers. He seemed to be addressing George, but he was not looking at him as he said, "I talked to Frank Kandelin this morning. He has no idea who did the shooting." Alvarado finished with his belt and fished in a pocket for two silver coins, which he did not hand to Homer but put on the examination table. Now, finally, his black eyes went to George's face. "You have been treating her — has she said who she thought might have shot her?"

George felt color coming to his face. "No. She remembers almost nothing about being shot. She told me she can't imagine. She does not believe she has any enemies."

The handsome rancher's expression reflected a faint look of sardonic skepticism. "She has one such enemy, eh?"

The three of them moved to the parlor, where Alvarado picked up his hat, thanked Homer, nodded to them both, and closed the front door after himself.

Homer fished for a limp blue bandanna to mop his eyes with. He had a headache and was fretful. "Every time lately someone comes in you aren't here."

George ignored that. "Have you eaten?"

"No."

"Come along. I'll fry something for you."

When they were in the kitchen, old Homer watched his associate in silence a moment, his head cocked a little. "George, I'm beginning to suspect that your interest in Maria Antonia's shooting is more than professional."

George had his back to Homer. "It's a puzzle, Homer, and I'm fascinated by puzzles," he said without turning around.

Hudspeth felt for his blue handkerchief again. "I didn't mean the shooting, I meant Maria Antonia the woman."

This time George turned. Homer missed his stare because his head was lowered as he mopped at his watering eyes. George turned back to his cooking. "She simply would not be the least bit interested in a pill roller who doesn't even own two suits of clothing or a good pair of boots."

Homer acknowledged this by bobbing his head. Then he said, "I wasn't talking about her being interested in you, George; I was talking about you . . ."

The younger physician was putting two fried eggs and a slab of ham onto a plate. He finished doing that and brought the plate to the table for Homer, smiling into Homer's pale eyes as he said, "I think she's the most beautiful woman I've ever seen. That's not professional, is it? But I am a man, Homer. As for involvement, I can't imagine anything more soul-fulfilling than to have a personal involvement with her, but it has not happened, and it won't happen. I'm her physician, she is my patient. That's all. Put some pepper on the ham, it's too bland otherwise."

Homer dutifully reached for the pepper grinder. "You are adapting, George," he said, putting it aside. "Pepper on country ham. Next you'll be eating *entamotados* for breakfast and *carne con chili* for supper."

A light but rapid knocking echoed from the front door. Homer looked around, but George put a hand on his shoulder. "Eat. I'll get it."

Homer growled as he went back to his meal. "Babies. They never arrive at a good time."

But it was not a frantic husband, it was that lean youth who had been out at the mission night before last. His eyes were enormous and he was clutching an old straw hat as though his intention was to demolish it. In rapid Spanish he told George he should come immediately to the mission. Father O'Malley had not appeared for early mass. When the youth had looked in on him, Father O'Malley was still in bed. The youth did not believe he was breathing.

George went after his hat and satchel and left Homer placidly at breakfast. The youth did not say a word on the way out to the mission. He almost seemed incapable of speaking.

The morning was another magnificently cool and subtly fragrant precursor of the heat yet to come. Beyond the mission to the northwest two old men riding over the hips of small burros were taking a mixed band of sheep and goats to graze the open country. Closer, someone was approaching town from the northeast, driving a top-buggy that had once been shiny black but which now was a lusterless shade of dead gray.

The moment they reached the long tiled concourse the youth put his hat on. While he had been in the sun he had clutched it. Now that he did not need protection from the sun he put it on.

When they reached the door to Father O'Malley's little room, which was ajar, the youth refused to go any farther. He took up a position along the wall, close enough to hear if anything was said inside but not near enough to see in there.

George pushed the door wide open to let in as much light as possible. He stopped at the bedside, looking at the peaceful, calm face of the man in the bed. His knees weakened, and he had to pull up the little three-legged stool and sit down. He did not need to listen for a heartbeat nor feel for a pulse.

He sat hunched and silent for a long time, then leaned forward to gently lift one eyelid. It would not completely close afterward; he gently forced it closed. *El Visitadoré* – death, "the visitor," had come and gone.

They had been friends. More, they had shared a variety of wry humor. George left the stool and went to a chair to sit. The entire community would mourn this loss. Father O'Malley had once told George that Lordsville had been without a priest for three years before he had arrived there. That was because the church had to consider the financial drain of maintaining the old mission, which was not exactly costly, but in a poor diocese all expenses had to be weighed carefully, and reweighed. In the end, O'Malley had been sent here to serve out his time in the Good Services. The reason? He had volunteered to serve without even a pittance and to restore the old mission as best he could, relying upon meager donations of money and the willingness of the faithful to do hard work for no pay.

George smiled to himself in the cool, shady little room. Father O'Malley had worked wonders. The old chapel had been roofless; it now had a good roof. A collapsed well had been redug by volunteer labor. The very old mission cemetery had been scourged of every weed, the stones straightened, new trees planted to give shade in place of the old diseased and dying trees.

The smile faded as George saw that earthen wine jug still on top of the dresser with a pair of sticky cups beside it. What in the hell had Homer been thinking of!

He stood up, leaned down to pull a bedcover gently over Father O'Malley's face, and returned to the tiled loggia, where the youth watched his every move without saying a word.

George looked at him. "There will be somebody," he said softly, "who served the altar with him. Ask him to see that the office of this diocese is notified of Father O'Malley's death, and ask him to make burial arrangements."

The youth nodded and moved soundlessly away on bare feet.

George closed the door and started back to

town. It was still a magnificent morning, something he was in no mood to appreciate. Before he reached the warped little picket fence in front of the Hudspeth house he paused to range an uninterested gaze down through town.

There were shoppers entering and leaving the emporium; farther south but on the same side of the road, either the blacksmith or his helper was shaping a huge freight wagon tire with heat and a large hammer.

Marshal Kandelin was leaning on an overhang upright down in front of the jailhouse in desultory conversation with a man George did not recognize, and two boys with sticks were rolling a discarded steel tire from a light buggy through roadway dust in front of the saddle and harness works. They were being trailed by a muscular medium-size spotted dog, tongue lolling.

Homer spoke from the doorway. "What was it, another baby?"

George regarded the beefy older man, whose jowls had begun to look puffy lately, and walked up through the gateway to the porch. He shouldered past to the parlor and put his satchel on a chair. "It was that youth from the mission. I don't know his name but —"

"Joaquin Sandoval," stated Homer, closing the door and coming into the parlor. "What did he want? Not a baby — he's only sixteen or seventeen, and he's not even married."

George said, "It was Father O'Malley."

Homer's breath came out slowly. "Ah. Too much wine, eh?"

"He is dead."

Homer was motionless for five seconds, then he looked around for a place to sit as though his legs had abruptly lost the ability to support his heavy bulk. He groped unconsciously for the limp blue handkerchief, but instead of wiping his eyes with it he sat balling it between his hands and looking at something between his chair and the parlor wall.

"What was it," he asked in a throaty whisper, "his heart?"

George considered the old man. "Yes, it was his heart." It had to be the heart — it was always the heart, regardless of what else it had been, because unless the heart stopped a man did not die.

Homer squeezed the blue handkerchief without meeting his associate's gaze. "I know what you're doing, George," he said in a whispery voice, and stopped balling the blue handkerchief. Homer pushed himself up out of the chair, heading for the kitchen. George remained where he had been, moving only when he heard liquid splashing into a glass. He went out front and sat on the porch, oblivious of the rising heat. He sat out there for a half hour, considering Lordsville, its people, the countryside, all of which he had grown fond of — especially the town, with its huge old trees and dusty roadway and the rangeland that ran in all directions around it.

He saw everything as it would be thirty, forty, perhaps even fifty years from now. There would be almost no change — except in himself, if he remained. If he did, unless he were capable of moving mountains of ignorance and superstition, the South Desert would beat him, as it had beaten Homer Hudspeth.

A very pretty girl with a complexion of old ivory, midnight black hair, and eyes almost that black turned in at the gate and walked toward the house. George's thoughts came slowly back to the present. The girl stopped ten feet distant and spoke gravely. "You are Dr. Brunner?"

George nodded.

"I am Guadalupe Gardea." At his blank look she added a little more. "I am the friend of the man whose wounded arm you took care of."

He looked more closely at her. "Walt Barnard?"

"*Sí.* Could I have a moment of your time, please?"

He patted the step he was sitting on.

"Will this be all right?"

She came up and sat beside him, clasping her hands as she leaned back slightly and gazed broodingly southward down Main Street. "You are his friend. He told me that. He said you were his only friend in Lordsville, except for my uncle, who lives over in Mex Town. I live with my uncle because we only have each other." She swung a long-lashed timid look in George's direction.

He wanted to put her at ease, so he said, "I'm glad you came. He told me a little about you." Then George looked into the delicate and lovely face and got a bad sensation in the pit of his stomach. But he held his small smile. "Is there illness? Something I can do?"

"You can. My uncle said there is no reason why you would do this, but you can go out to the Alvarado ranch and ask him to quit."

George's stomach knotted. He stared. "The Alvarado place? Walt Barnard? But I thought he had gone south to the border."

"No, Doctor. He went partway, then came back. He rode around town to find the Alvarado ranch, and they hired him as a rider. I know because last night he came in the dark and made a night bird whistle outside my window."

George glanced quickly away, and saw Marshal Kandelin talking to that vinegary old clerk at the general store. Having the massive, cold-eyed lawman in sight did not make him feel any better. He turned back to Guadalupe Gardea. "Why did he . . . ?" It was an asinine question. Gaudalupe Gardea was beautiful, with a gentle, kind and caring soul that shone from her dark eyes. "Never mind. All right. I'll go out tomorrow, if I can, and talk to him. But the priest died last night, so I may not be able to."

Both the girl's hands flew to her mouth. "Padre O'Malley — is dead?"

"Yes. The funeral may be tomorrow. If not, then I'll go hunt up Walt."

The lovely girl had tears in her eyes as she rose from the step. "He was so good to us over in Mex Town, Doctor."

George nodded. "To everyone, señorita."

"I will go now," she said, keeping tight control. "You will talk to Walt?"

"Yes. I'll do my best to get him to leave the country. But," George said, showing his frank admiration, "I don't believe that if I were Walt, I'd go without you."

She left him, walking briskly down to the gate and over across the road toward one of the numerous dogtrots between the stores in Gringo Town, which ended over in Mex Town.

CHAPTER 9

BEARING TIDINGS

Despite having eaten breakfast Homer still had a terrible headache. He complained of it to George, who told him what to take. George was called to the front door by a grizzled, very dark old Mexican, whose white hair made him appear even darker. He smiled deferentially and pulled off his straw hat when George faced him.

George thought he had seen this old man before, and remembered two old herders riding burros the day before, driving their mixed band of sheep and goats. The old man said in Spanish that Father O'Malley's funeral would be tomorrow, at sunrise. George thanked him and closed the door as the old man shuffled away.

Homer was in the parlor. He had heard every

word and met George's gaze with what seemed to be an unfocused directness. He nodded that he knew, and walked out of the room.

George's heart ached for the old man, whose irresponsibility had contributed to the death of his friend, the priest.

There was nothing more that he could say or do, so he got his hat and went down to the livery barn for his sorrel horse. He knew where the headquarters of the Alvarado ranch was, but he had an idea that if he could find Walt Barnard away somewhere, out on the range, it would be better for them both, so when he left town he did so on an angling course, which would put him on Alvarado land but not in the direction of the yard.

It was still refreshingly cool, and while riding George raised his eyes to the vastness of the land, with its lifts and swales, its ageless soft silence, its seemingly eternal beauty and abundance. He had a feeling for this broad strip of open land lying between more northerly areas of bitter winters and blazing summers and the southerly country, where the true South Desert began and continued for hundreds of miles, down across the border into the hostile desert areas of Mexico's Chihuahua and Sonora provinces.

He thought of many things: the shooting of

Maria Antonia, of the beautiful woman herself; of Homer and Father O'Malley; of the lovely, gentle girl named after Guadalupe, the heroine saint of Mexico; of the gunman with his ivory-stocked six-gun he was going to meet today; of his own position in the midst of all this. George told his horse with an almost sad gravity that he would not leave this country, although he most certainly should.

The sorrel as usual did not pay the slightest attention to the voice of its rider. Its attention had already been fixed on something even before the two-legged thing on its back had spoken.

Five horsemen loping westward about two miles dead ahead. Too far to distinguish anything about them except the fact that they were mounted men.

George reined down into a swale and stopped to watch. That they were Carter Alvarado's riders he had no doubt. Whether one of them would be Walt Barnard, he had no idea. At any rate this possibility did not please him; he wanted to meet Walt when he had no companions.

He thought that Alvarado, like the other traditionalists in this territory, would have a number of vaqueros to work his herds. Some ranchers, as old David Lord had been able to do if an emergency required it, could put fifteen or twenty vaqueros on horseback in less than an hour. If this applied to Carter Alvarado, then what George was watching would be perhaps less than half of his riders, and that decreased the odds of Walt Barnard being among the distant horsemen.

He sat and watched until the horsemen were dim and small in the distance. Deciding there was a better way to accomplish his purpose, he turned back southwest and rode in solemn thought until he had the stage road in sight. He altered course slightly, crossed the road, and boosted the sorrel over into a rocking-chair lope, holding him to it until his neck darkened with sweat, and finally hauling him down to a steady walk.

The coolness was being replaced by oppressive heat. He noticed this and squinted at the position of the sun. It was nearing midday.

By the time he had the huge old trees and rooftops of the Lord yard in sight, his horse's shadow was directly beneath him.

The yard was silent, seemingly empty. Among the adobe jacals there was some sign of life, but not much. In the middle of the day this had no significance; people were preparing for the heat.

After he had left his horse in the barn and

had returned to the yard, it occurred to him that the heat was different today. It seemed more oppressive, less dry than usual. He paused to look upward. Those massive and mountainous white clouds he had seen a day or two earlier were now well forward of the farthest horizon, advancing majestically toward Lordsville. They seemed not to be moving at all, but that was an illusion. The rain he had anticipated several days ago was inexorably on its way. Maybe it would not arrive tonight or tomorrow, but it would come.

He went to the big house and was crossing the patio when the oaken front door swung back to allow Juan Esteven to emerge. He did not see Dr. Brunner until he had put on his hat, then he blinked in surprise. He closed the door at his back and said, *"Buenas días."*

George nodded and responded in English. "Good morning. I didn't see you in the yard — I thought you'd be out there with the riders."

Esteven walked closer. "I would have been, but the lady wanted to discuss ranch matters." Juan's black eyes smiled shrewdly. In Spanish he said, "You are to her a matter of interest, friend." Then he nodded and walked on out of the patio.

George rapped lightly on the door, half expecting the voluptuous girl with the ribbons in her hair. Instead the door was opened by Doña Teresa Maria, whose level, no-nonsense gaze was neither hostile nor friendly as she stepped aside and closed the door behind him. This time, though, she did not take him down the domed corridor but said, "You must tell her she cannot leave the bed."

He considered the erect, angular older woman. "I will."

"Good," she said and led the way.

Maria Antonia had been bathed, her black hair had been dressed by someone who was experienced at doing this, and when George entered the bedroom, fragrance from the open window reached him immediately. Maria Antonia had the full golden color which was normal to her, and although she did not smile at the doctor, she said, "I have been waiting."

He fished for the gold watch, flipped it open, and took her pulse. Without speaking, he put up the watch and leaned down to listen to her heartbeat. As he was straightening up, he smiled. She said, "Good, Doctor?"

"Very good, but you can't get out of bed yet."

"When can I?"

He pulled a chair around and sat down before answering, aware of Doña Teresa Maria's black eyes fixed on him.

"*Quién sabe?*" he replied, and grinned.

Maria Antonia ignored the grin. She was impatient. "If you don't know," she told him in English, "make a guess."

"Possibly in three weeks."

The black eyes did not move from his face. "Doctor, listen to my breathing."

He did not leave the chair. For a moment they looked steadily at each other, then he said, "Do you know what doctors have to face with everyone they treat? No? I'll explain something to you, then. To start with, the lungs have very little feeling. If you stub your toe, even though it's not serious it will cause excruciating pain. Lungs can be shot through and the actual sensation of pain is less than if you'd had a stomachache. But they heal very slowly. And they are susceptible to hemorrhage and pneumonia. It is going to rain in a day or two. If you aren't very careful, you could catch a simple cold, which, in your condition, could kill you. I want you to heal completely. You've got to stay in this bed and keep that window closed – I know. I know you feel strong. Everyone does who has been ill, especially people who have been confined to a bed for any length of time. Will you promise me to stay in bed?"

The beautiful woman glanced briefly at her aunt, then toward the window, with its inviting warm fragrance and its view of shimmering heat over miles of grassland. "Three weeks, Doctor?"

"Maybe even longer," he said. He leaned forward. "Father O'Malley died last night."

As a distraction, it got even more of a reaction from the women than he had thought it might. Aunt Teresa Maria, who had always remained as erectly upright as a sentinel when George was in the bedroom, sank into a chair. Maria Antonia's head came around slowly, dark eyes round and bright with shock.

He sat waiting. It was Teresa Maria who finally spoke. "But . . . he was not an old man."

George nodded in silence.

The older woman looked at the clasped hands in her lap. She was not only very religious, she also possessed an inherent fatalism. God was good, and when He caused anguish, it was to be borne. What people could not change, they must accept in good grace – it was His will.

Maria Antonia made a quiet inquiry. "Did he die in peace, Doctor?"

George thought he had. There certainly had been no indication that he had died otherwise; no rigid muscles, no contorted features, none of the straining neck muscles or the head turned as far as it could turn, none of the terrible grimacing that commonly went with a death from poisoning.

"I think he died at peace in his sleep," he replied.

Teresa Maria looked up. "The funeral, Doctor?"

"Tomorrow at sunrise, señora. At the old mission." He looked at Maria Antonia. "You stay."

The beautiful woman looked back toward the window. George got to his feet before she looked at him again. He leaned down to touch her hand. Their eyes met and held. He checked the impulse to repeat his statement that she was not to leave the bed. He left the room, encountering no one until he got down to the barn. As before, the mayordomo just happened to be leaning in the shade of the barn, waiting for him.

Juan Esteven helped in the bridling and saddling. As he did this he said, "She has a very strong will. Like her father."

George let down the stirrup leather on the left side after tightening the latigo. "Did you see those big clouds?" he replied.

Esteven nodded, looking bewildered. They had not been discussing clouds.

"It's going to rain, Juan. If she leaves the house — if only to talk to you in the yard — and is chilled, she can come down with pneumonia, and it would probably kill her."

Esteven's face cleared. "*Sí.* Well, what can anyone do? I said she has her father's will. There is no one here who can give her an order. You understand?"

George caught up the reins and led his horse out of the barn. "She may want to drive to Lordsville early tomorrow morning."

Both men stepped out into hot sunshine. Juan Esteven raised his brows. "Why would she want to do that, amigo?"

George turned the sorrel once, mounted him, and evened up the reins as he replied. "Because Father O'Malley died last night and his funeral will be at sunrise tomorrow morning, at the old mission."

George nodded and reined around to ride out of the yard. The mayordomo seemed rooted in place as he stared after the departing rider. It took longer for the shock to pass in the yard than it had in the house. George was half a mile out before the stunned mayordomo made the sign of the cross over his thick chest and turned to go into the barn.

The shock George had left behind him was the same degree of shock he had felt when he had entered the gloomy, spartan little room at the mission where he had realized that Father O'Malley had died. While the people back at the ranch were still too stunned to think of other things, George rode toward town lost in considerations that did not bear directly upon the passing of the priest. He'd had half a day to recover. The people he had left behind would need at least that much time.

He speculated upon Maria Antonia's reaction. Of Doña Teresa Maria he had no doubt; he was certain that if she were the one in bed gravely ill but rational she would force a weak body to leave the bed, dress, go to the yard, demand that a buggy be hitched up, and drive to the mission through miles of early morning cold to attend the funeral — perhaps to collapse afterward, be put to bed with a raging fever, and die.

Maria Antonia had never impressed George as possessing the religious fervor of her aunt. He wondered if Maria Antonia's more rational approach was something she had inherited from her father. From what George knew of David Lord and from what he had heard about him, while he supported the mission unstintingly, David Lord's obsession had been his ranch, not his faith. George was within sight of the Lordsville rooftops when he decided that since Maria Antonia was so much like her dead father and had certainly been greatly influenced by him, she probably would not attempt anything rash.

He certainly hoped so.

The sorrel horse had been plodding along on loose reins, sweating heavily in the shimmering heat. Now he abruptly threw his head up, little ears pointing toward a distant swale. George came out of his reverie to tip down his hat and squint in the same direction.

He saw nothing, but his horse, who probably had not seen anything either, had definitely picked up a scent. Without changing leads or drifting off course to approach nearer to the swale, the sorrel continued to be curious, and that, in an animal who was of a breed whose attention span was very brief even in the presence of actual danger, aroused his rider's interest too.

The afternoon was at its peak. Anything in the middle distance was subject to shimmery heat-haze distortion. George knew that swale; it was fairly wide and deep. He considered the possibility of a calving cow being down in there; cows would leave a herd if they could to go off and calve by themselves. He doubted that it would be horses; they would have picked up the sorrel's scent and come changing up the near side of the swale to stand and stare.

It was neither a cow nor loose stock, it was a horseman. He appeared on the edge of the swale and sat as motionless as stone, watching George approach. Heat haze distorted him, and the distance played tricks, too. George did not think he knew the rider. Beyond the still figure he could make out the stage road through the smokelike haze.

When he was less than two hundred yards from the horseman he recognized him. It was Marshal Frank Kandelin, his powerfully muscled upper body and unsmiling features, though shaded by his hat, unmistakable.

CHAPTER 10

SOMETHING UNEXPECTED

Kandelin reined northwestward toward a point of interception. George watched without any particular concern until they were close enough for him to raise a hand in salute. He called a greeting, which the lawman ignored as he sat his horse, blocking George's way.

George drew rein with a few yards separating them, studying the lawman's hard face with its bleak expression, and finally he began having misgivings. He said, "Were you looking for me? Is there something wrong in town?"

Instead of replying, Kandelin kneed his horse closer and halted with both gloved hands lying atop the saddle horn without taking his eyes off the doctor. The only thing he said was "Get down."

George did not move. He knew Kandelin,

but right now it was less what he knew about the man than what he had heard about him that seemed to matter. Kandelin's little gun-metal eyes were squeezed nearly closed, his mouth was pursed and flattened. He looked particularly ugly.

He leaned forward slightly in his saddle. "I said, 'Get down!' "

George still did not move. "Do you want to explain?" he asked. Marshal Kandelin dismounted, and while trailing the rawhide split-reins of his own horse, stepped forward to grasp the sorrel's reins about six inches behind the curbstrap. "Get down or I'll pull you down," he said.

George kicked his right boot free and dismounted. They were no more than six or seven feet apart when Marshal Kandelin released his grip on the sorrel's reins, eyeing George through slits, and methodically tugged on the cuffs of his riding gloves. Then he moved.

He was very fast for a man of his build. No doubt this had been responsible for his triumph in other physical encounters. He was fast on his feet and even faster with his fists. George saw only a blur before the blow landed, then he felt hard ground and dimly perceived his startled sorrel horse from the underside.

He heaved awkwardly to one side and pushed

himself up. He could taste blood on his lips. When he was standing again he felt for the sorrel to support him. The horse moved uneasily away and George nearly fell.

The second blow sank wrist-deep into his unprotected soft parts, and this time he fell forward on his face. He could not breathe, even though his torn mouth was sprung wide. A tiny amount of air returned to his lungs. His vision was impaired. He could see objects, like the widespread legs of Marshal Kandelin, but it was like seeing them under water.

He was roughly wrenched upright by a powerful arm and held like a broken rag doll as Marshal Kandelin snarled something George could not understand. The second strike in the stomach arrived as Frank Kandelin released his grip. This time when George fell on his face there was almost no sensation of pain, but he vomited.

Marshal Kandelin stepped back, flung off sweat, resettled his hat on his head, tugged again on his gloves, and stood watching. George had greater difficulty this time pushing himself back off the ground. He could not stand. He raised himself partially up, but his sense of equilibrium failed. He toppled sideways and lay like that, blood from his mouth across one side of his face. He tried dumbly and desperately to catch his breath.

Marshal Kandelin stood in the partial shade of his horse, continuing to watch. Once he turned to look backward and to his right, then he looked down again, as Dr. Brunner fought for breath.

When he could get it, he sucked in great amounts of air, and after a few moments that helped. He could get up onto all fours, but had no strength to do any more. He hung there, dripping blood and sweat, his shirt torn and soiled. He was sick again.

Kandelin sank to one knee. He was completely shaded by his horse when he did this. He lifted his hat and used a red bandana to mop his sweat with. Replacing the hat and stuffing the handkerchief into a hip pocket, he said, "You listen to me. Barnard don't matter. I know you talked to him at the livery barn. The day man told me, an' when I got down there lookin' for him he was gone. I could have locked you up for that, George. But that ain't it. Can you understand what I'm saying?" When George did not answer Kandelin leaned down to grab his shirt, forcing George's head up. "Answer me you son-of-a-bitch, or I'll tear your head off. Do you understand what I'm saying?"

George nodded. He understood, but Kandelin's voice sounded a long way off, and his fierce, flushed, sweat-dripping face was indistinct.

Kandelin released his grip and George nearly fell. Kandelin waited until he was on all fours before he spoke. "You butted in where you had no business with Barnard. But that's not why I was waitin' out here for you. I know where you been because I watched you. First, you went northeast, then you changed course and went in a beeline to the Lord place. Now you listen to me. You been askin' questions out there, and in town too. You're goin' to get yourself killed, and ol' Hudspeth right along with you — because sure as hell you been talkin' to him too. Raise your head. Look at me!"

George made the effort. He felt sick, but his hearing was improving. Along with it his vision had cleared sufficiently so that he could see Marshal Kandelin's savage expression.

"You leave things be, George. Quit askin' questions. Quit even thinkin' about Maria Antonia gettin' shot. You hear me? Stick to your doctoring. Mind your own damn business, because if we hear just one more story of you askin' questions about that shootin' you're goin' to just up and disappear, and no one'll ever even find your bones."

Marshal Kandelin used his red handkerchief

again and stood up. "An' when you make it back to town — if you do, an' I don't give a damn either way — you remember our little visit out here. If ol' Hudspeth asks what happened to your face, you fell off your horse in some rocks. You understand me, George? There won't be no second warning." Kandelin turned down along the left side of his horse, toed in, and rose up to come down across leather. He sat briefly, considering the man he had mercilessly beaten, then reined around and rode southward, parallel to the town, which was wrapped in heat haze to the east. He evidently had planned this ambush right down to riding back into town from the lower stage road.

George's stomach hurt, his mouth was swollen, his eyes and throat burned. He eased flat down and did not move until the sorrel horse came over and nudged him, then he reached for one rein and held it until he could sit up. The sun had moved a fair distance down the western sky. He deduced from this that he had either lost consciousness or had slept for at least two hours.

He pulled himself upright by using the stirrup and stirrup leather. He leaned on the horse until he felt strong enough to drag himself into the saddle. He failed twice. The third time he got astride, and the moment he was in place up there the sorrel horse started walking. He was thirsty.

George clung to the saddle horn. He was hatless, and the sun struck his bare head on a slanting angle. He rocked with the horse, which made him think he was going to vomit again, but he didn't. As his mind began to clear, he looked around for landmarks. The sorrel had not headed directly for town, which George had expected him to do, but had gone northward in the direction of the stage road. When this became clear to George the horse was crossing the road, still walking eastward when he should have been traveling south, down through town in the direction of the livery barn, where he knew there was feed, shade, and water.

In fact, the sorrel was following a scent of water. He went along with sagging reins until he was near the mission, then turned south. George's mind was clearing fast by now. He was ill and feeble and unsteady in the saddle, and he also became peevishly irritable and would have yanked the horse around if he'd had the strength. Instead he swore at it through swollen lips, and as always the sorrel gave no heed to the sounds made by the two-legged thing on its back.

George was riding head-hung. He did not

feel the horse slacken, seem to hesitate. Nor did he hear someone speak in startled Spanish, not even when a second voice was also raised in astonishment. He was only aware of one thing, he was falling. It seemed to take forever before the ground came up to him. He lost consciousness.

When consciousness returned it was dark except for the soft light of three yellow candles, each in a little separate dish. He was on a narrow wall bunk. The mattress beneath him was filled with dry corn husks, and each time he moved even his head the mattress made busy little rustling sounds.

He could see clearly. He recognized the dark old man with white hair standing beside the bed looking down at him. It was the same man who had come to tell him when Father O'Malley's funeral would be. The other old man was smaller, even darker and more wrinkled. Between them stood the beautiful girl he remembered from sitting with her on the steps at Homer's house. By candlelight she looked even younger and more lovely. She leaned closer and spoke to him in Spanish. She was holding a small gourd. "You must drink," she said, and held the gourd closer to his face. "You have been sick. This is the curandera's medicine for your stomach."

The old man with white hair knelt and raised George by the shoulders. He showed a kindly smile. "Drink," he said in Spanish.

George drank. For several moments he did not believe the liquid was going to stay down, but it did. The girl used a wet rag on his face. The coolness helped a lot. She had already wiped away the blood and had treated his torn mouth with something that smelled powerfully of sheep. His mouth did not hurt, and after a few minutes his battered stomach also felt better.

The old man who had supported him wagged his head and spoke again in Spanish. "Doctor, you were injured. How did this happen?"

George lay back, breathing deeply. That also helped clear his mind, increased his sense of recovery. "Fell off my horse," he said through swollen lips, and the two old Mexicans exchanged a knowing look. The white-headed man raised a skeptical eyebrow. "Three times, señor?" At the look George put on him the old man shrugged. "Once in the mouth, señor, two times very hard in the stomach?"

The old men padded silently out of the room, leaving him with the lovely girl. She brought a bench to his bedside and sat on it, looking at him. He asked about his horse. She said, "He smelled the water my uncle and his friend filled the goat trough with. He was very thirsty, and you fell off when he put his head down to drink. They brought you in here. The horse is in a faggot pen and has been fed. . . . Doctor, what was it? Who did it?"

He raised a hand to gingerly probe his mouth and did not answer. He remembered everything clearly, which was surprising, because after being knocked down the first time his mind had not seemed clear at all. He even remembered every word Marshal Kandelin had said, and as he was examining his mouth to determine the extent of the damage, he particularly remembered one particular sentence: *Mind your own damn business, because if we hear just one more story about you askin' questions* . . . He stared at the girl. "We?" he said.

She regarded him with curiosity, ignoring what he had said, and asked a question. "It wasn't Walt, was it? No, I can't believe it was him. You are his friend."

George's mind returned to something he had considered much earlier, very early this morning, in fact, when he had been watching those five vaqueros over on Alvarado's range. He had decided that rather than ride himself sore trying to catch Walt alone he would simply come to this house after nightfall and wait for Walt to appear.

He said, "No, it wasn't Walt," and paused, looking steadily at her for a moment. "Guadalupe, you told me he came in the night."

"Yes."

"Will he come tonight?"

The candlelight was too weak for him to see the color come into her face, but when she turned to avoid his eyes he understood, and without waiting for her to reply he said, "I want to talk to him."

She nodded, probably believing his wanting to see Walt had to do with what she had asked him to do; insist that Walt leave the country.

George was not thinking of that at all. "I want very much to see him, to talk to him."

She nodded again, still avoiding his gaze, and rose from the bench and went to the doorless opening, where she turned. "You sleep. Later, I will feed you, but for now you need sleep," she said.

He needed something. Among other things he needed to get word to Homer, but most of all he needed to know who the "we" was Marshal Kandelin had mentioned.

As for Kandelin himself, one thing stood out glaringly. He knew more about the shooting of Maria Antonia than George had thought. In fact, George had attributed Kandelin's lack of interest in the shooting to characteristic gringo lack of concern when natives were shot. Kandelin would not be the only individual in the Lordsville country who felt this way.

"We" implied a lot more than George had suspected. "We" implied that there had perhaps been some kind of conspiracy about the shooting of Maria Antonia. What George was thinking about just before he fell asleep was the extent of that conspiracy, and the probable reason for it. Lord's Land was an empire. If it became ownerless, the conspirators — of which George was certain Frank Kandelin was one — would stake their claim.

He was beginning to feel a dawning anxiety for Maria Antonia's welfare when the drowsiness rose like a wall in his mind. He had several seconds to wonder what the curandera had put into that stomach medicine before he went to sleep.

A dog barked somewhere north of the jacal, otherwise Mex Town was quiet. Echoing boisterousness from over in Gringo Town reached the warm-night squatting places, where resting people were visible under sagging *ramadas* by the red tips of cigarettes rolled from brown wheat-straw papers.

Elizondo Gardea trickled smoke from his mouth and gazed in the direction of the empty plaza, which had a deep, partially bricked-up well where people drew water during daylight, and listened to his old friend, the smaller, sinewy old man. When the talking stopped Gardea removed his cigarette and without taking his eyes off the large, low, circular brick wall around the well, he said. "One man does not beat another man that badly unless he thinks he has good reason, old friend. I think the doctor should own a gun."

"Or," stated his friend dryly, "saddle up and leave the country."

Elizondo Gardea's strong white teeth showed in the darkness. "Yes. Or leave the country. But this is a man who will not do that."

"No. You are sure, then?"

Gardea was about to reply but cocked his head at the sound of a slow-walking horse. He leaned quickly to stub out his smoke and arose. "Come, companion. We are not to be here when the horseman slips into town to see my niece."

The old men faded among shadows on their way toward the crude but efficient faggot pens they owned together. Out there, with an overpowering smell of sheep and goats, they had a stoneware jug wrapped in burlap buried in the ground to keep its contents cool.

CHAPTER 11

TROUBLESOME
THOUGHTS

Guadalupe brought Walt Barnard to the small, softly lit room and left him there looking solemnly down at the man on the cot with the swollen mouth and soiled clothing. She returned to the cooking area to prepare food for George. She was by nature discreet and tactful.

Walt pulled a bench over, dropped down onto it, shoved back his hat, hitched the holstered six-gun around, leaning forward as he said, "You look like you been kicked by a mule, Doctor."

George considered the bronzed, strong features. As always, Walt's blue eyes looked more blue in their darkly tanned setting. Instead of starting their conversation where he thought it should begin, George said, "I can guess why you came back, but it wasn't a very wise thing to do."

Walt did not dispute that. "Like I told you, doctor," he replied, "I thought I saw a glimmer of hope for a decent life in a place where no one would ever know me, and with a woman I've never met the equal of." Barnard raised and lowered wide, strong shoulders. "If I'd gone down over the line I'd have returned to her anyway, so why should I go?"

"Because Marshal Kandelin has a Nebraska dodger on you. The reward is five hundred dollars. Five hundred, dead or alive. Kandelin told me he didn't care which it was. Walt, that's not going to help Guadalupe Gardea one damn bit."

Barnard leaned back slightly on the bench. He eyed George's lopsided face for a long time before speaking again. "Doctor, I'm going to tell you something I shouldn't."

"Then don't," exclaimed George, who did not relish the idea of keeping any more secrets.

As though he had not spoken, Walt continued in the same quiet, drawling voice. "Kandelin don't know I'm back, and he won't know unless he comes right up face to face with me. I work for a feller who's got reason for not liking Kandelin."

George said, "Carter Alvarado?"

Walt nodded without asking how George

136

knew who he was working for; he had more to say on a subject that was fixed strongly in his mind to the exclusion of anything else. "Alvarado and his remudero were on the west range looking for horses. They were maybe a mile and a half across the stage road. That's Lord land over there but the remudero told me that wasn't the first time they'd had to go over there for strays. They didn't find the horses. They hunted up shade and rested for a spell. They saw a lot of horseback and buggy traffic goin' from town out to the Lord ranch yard. That was the day old man Lord was to be buried."

George eased himself up gently until he was propping himself with one arm. He had a very strong premonition.

Walt got more comfortable on the crude old wooden bench before continuing. "They had some cold *chorizo* and water, so they ate and relaxed for a while. About the time they was ready to cinch up and head for home, their horses got interested in something a considerable distance away. There was a rider north of the trees where they was sitting. He was riding pretty fast for the kind of a day it was, so they walked back through the trees to see him better. When he passed the trees he was about a mile north. A little later, when he was past, he commenced to angle southward in the direction of Lordville."

Walt paused, and George said, "What time of day was it?"

Walt gave a wolfish smile. "Mr. Alvarado guessed it was maybe fifteen minutes after the lady at the cemetery got shot. Only they hadn't heard anything and didn't know there had been a shooting, so they stood back in the trees watching the feller go past." Walt Barnard paused again, leaning forward slightly and looking George straight in the eye. "He was carrying a long-barreled Winchester rifle across his lap. There wasn't no boot on his saddle, but if there had been, the rifle would have been too long to fit in it."

George eased back down. "He was too far for them to recognize, Walt?"

"Well, Mr. Alvarado thinks he recognized him but the remudero says it wasn't that man."

"What man?"

"You know a mean-mouthed liveryman in town?"

George turned his face toward the rangeman. Walt nodded his head slowly. "Him. But the ranch horseman says the man they saw was a Mexican, not a gringo. Anyway, Mr. Alvarado went to town to talk to Marshal Kandelin, and the lawman laughed at him — wouldn't do anythin' and said he was makin' an investigation that would eventually turn up the bushwhacker. Mr. Alvarado's not a feller you'd ought to laugh at."

Guadalupe came hesitantly to the doorway and was beckoned forward. George hoisted himself up and ate hot broth, tortillas, and a faintly sweet thick pudding made of maize, and drank half a glass of red wine.

She smiled at him, encouraged by his appetite. "If you will give me your clothes, I will clean them," she said.

George declined the offer with thanks. He told her he had to leave, to let Doctor Hudspeth know he was all right. He was certain that by now Homer would be very worried.

She looked shyly at Walt, and when she left the room Walt trailed after her.

After George had rested an additional half hour, he sat up on the edge of the bunk, and when no pain or dizziness arrived, he stood up. His stomach dully ached, but otherwise he felt capable enough to leave.

There was no sign of the two old men on the meager front porch, with its earthen floor as hard as stone, and he was aiming toward one of the dogtrots which led to Main Street in Gringo Town when a quiet voice halted him.

"Doctor, you never told me about the mule

that kicked you." Walt strolled from shadows near the rear of the house, thumbs hooked in his shell belt, head slightly tilted. He stopped, seeming to await an answer, and when none came he spoke again. "That wasn't no mule, that was a man who did that to you. I'm a real curious feller, Doctor. Who was he?"

George did not hesitate. "The man your boss doesn't like."

Walt showed no surprise. "Why, Doctor?"

"It's a long story, Walt, and I have to get —"

"Doctor, you're fine at patching nail gashes, but I'd say maybe I'm better at knowin' about men. If Kandelin did that to you, he had a reason, an' if you go up through that dog-trot and he's still feelin' mean, or maybe has been drinkin', I wouldn't give a plugged centavo for your chances of ever getting home. Why did he do it? We got plenty of time, Doctor."

"I've been trying to find out who shot Maria Antonia Lord. I guess I asked more questions than I should have. When I was riding back to town he was waiting out there for me. He told me if I didn't mind my own business I'd wind up dead."

"And," stated the lanky rangeman, "he overhauled your workings to make his point."

George gave him a crooked smile. "Something like that."

"Doctor, how about ridin' out yonder and talkin' to Mr. Alvarado with me?"

George frowned. "Now?"

Walt seemed to have had another thought between the time he asked his question and George's answer. "Tell you what I think, Doctor. I think maybe Mr. Alvarado ought to come to town an' look you up." Walt smiled in the darkness. "Maybe fetch along the whole riding crew." Walt laughed softly, but George did not laugh at all. He knew just enough about Carter Alvarado to suspect that if he came to Lordsville with perhaps as many as twenty armed rangemen and Marshal Kandelin showed contempt for him again, there might very well be a battle on Main Street people would talk about for a hundred years.

He also thought of something else as he gazed at Walt Barnard. If Walt came to town with Carter Alvarado, Marshal Kandelin would try to lock Walt up. He said, "Let it go, Walt."

"We can't do that, Doctor."

"Why can't you? You haven't done anything about the mean-looking liveryman. If Alvarado is right, he's more to blame for the shooting of Maria Antonia Lord than Kandelin is."

Walt shifted his stance and glanced up through the dogtrot. He looked in the opposite direction, toward the rear of the adobe house.

"All right," he said finally. "Just Mr. Alvarado, Doctor. But if that lawman is watching you and sees you talkin' to Mr. Alvarado . . ."

George said, "I'll ride out before daybreak in the morning. I'll go straight north up the stage road. It'll look like Mr. Alvarado just happened to be riding in that direction too. . . . Walt, I'm worried about some of this."

Barnard inclined his head. He did not look worried, although he replied that he was. Then he winked, turned around, and headed toward the rear of the Gardea residence.

George walked up through the narrow opening between two wooden buildings and paused just inside the dogtrot to look both ways before stepping forth into Gringo Town. There was no more pedestrian traffic than usual this late at night. Most of the hitch racks were empty. A few places showed lights, such as the saloon, the pool hall, the jailhouse, and farther down, the livery barn.

There was piano music coming from the saloon. Whoever was playing was not very good, and the piano had not been tuned in five or six years, not since the last piano-tuner-and-tinkerer had passed through Lordsville.

George crossed the road heading for the Hudspeth place. When he walked in, Homer was getting ready for bed, but he came padding into the parlor as soon as he heard George. His jaw dropped. "What happened to you?" he asked.

"My horse dumped me in some rocks."

"Let's take a lamp into the examination room and look —"

"I'll be all right, Homer. It looks worse than it feels."

"Did you land on your face?"

George nodded.

"We better put some disinfectant on it, George."

"Maybe in the morning. Good night, Homer."

Homer stood his ground. "Not in the morning. The funeral is at sunrise."

"All right. In the afternoon. Good night."

"Did you eat?"

"Yes," George replied, walking. He stopped and turned around. "I'm tired and sore, Homer. I may not make it to the funeral in the morning."

The old doctor was sympathetic. "Sleep in. You look like you need rest. Don't worry about missing the funeral. Good night."

When George was in his room he peeled off his clothing. He waited a half hour, then went silently out to the kitchen, heated water, scrubbed, emptied the water into the geranium bed as usual and padded back to his room. The town was quiet now; even the off-key piano someone had been mauling at the saloon was silent.

He got into bed and watched reflected moonlight on the ceiling. By early morning, his restless mind had reflected on everything that had happened to him on this day. He recalled once hearing someone say that about two thirds of the time a man rose in the morning with no idea what he would go through before suppertime.

The previous day certainly had seemed to support that notion. George remained flat on his back for a long time, waiting for sleep. It did not come. It had arrived with unexpected swiftness at the Gardea place after he had taken that stomach medicine. He had slept like a log after that, and possibly that was the reason he could not sleep now.

Very gradually an idea occurred to him. The more he considered it, the more awake he became. Carter Alvarado and his ranch horseman had seen the man who had almost certainly been the ambusher who had tried to kill Maria Antonia Lord. They could not agree on his identity. The remudero had thought the gunman was a Mexican. Carter Alvarado had thought he was the Lordsville liveryman.

144

George sat up. The idea which had suddenly taken such a strong hold of him offered a solution to the disagreement between the rancher and his employee. The gunman could have been both – he could have been the liveryman dressed as a Mexican vaquero. In the South Desert country every rangeman wore the traditional attire of his trade. Vaqueros wore the large sombreros, short jackets and tight trousers of Mexico. Gringo riders dressed as all norteamericano rangemen dressed. They looked distinctly different from Mexican rangemen.

The Lord ranch had no gringo riders among its rangemen. In fact, a man dressed as a norteamericano cowboy would have aroused the interest of anyone who saw him out there the day old David Lord was buried. But a vaquero would not; all the Lord ranch riders dressed as vaqueros, and there were a large number of them on the ranch that day, but most were out at the cemetery, with their women, children, and old people.

George stood up, reaching for his trousers. He finished dressing, except for his hat, which was still on the ground out where he had met Marshal Kandelin. Then he went to the window to look down through town. The place looked deserted all the way to its southern end, where the last buildings, dimly lit now, stood on each side of the stage road where it ran straight south.

The back alley would be even more empty. It was not used very often, even in broad daylight. He went out to the parlor, hesitating as another thought occurred to him. Then he went over to a small closet, opened the door, and found the old shell belt and holstered Colt hanging there, which he took down. He had to pull the belt to its last notch when he buckled it around his waist, and even then it sagged.

Homer had told him he had not worn that gun in fifteen years. Because George felt uncomfortable wearing the belt and weapon, he returned to his room for a coat. It did a passable job of hiding the belt, but the sagging holster hung below it. There was nothing to be done about that.

George left the house by the rear door, reaching the alley, and turning south. He knew what he wanted to do, but he had no idea how to accomplish it until he had walked nearly the full length of town and could smell the livery barn straight ahead.

It was darker in the alley than it would have been around front on Main Street. As he hesitated near the barn's doorless rear opening, something passed overhead, blocking out what little light there was. He glanced upward. A mass of clouds had drifted in front of the moon and stars. Until this moment he had completely forgotten the prediction he had made to himself about the imminence of rain.

CHAPTER 12

IGNORING KANDELIN'S WARNING

The night man, a slight, older man, slept in the harness room. He was probably not as old as he looked, but he drank heavily. George had known him since his arrival in Lordsville. There was almost no likelihood of the night man being the rider Alvarado and his companion had seen. One reason was that he was too small. Another reason would be that as badly as his hands shook, he would not be capable of the ambusher's sharpshooting.

The mean-looking day man was much taller, thicker and younger, but George had no idea where he spent his nights, unless it was up at the Lordsville boardinghouse, which was where most of the unmarried men who worked in town had rooms.

If the day man lived at the rooming house,

George's chance of finding vaquero attire at the barn seemed slim, but since he had to begin his search somewhere, he entered the barn. The darkness increased with each step he took. Several stalled horses moved drowsily on straw, and one thrust his head over the lower half of the stall door, wide awake and interested. George ignored him.

The harness room door was open and someone was snoring wetly in the darkness beyond. Geroge stopped close to the doorway.

Opposite the harness room was a small room used for storing feed grain. George began his search over there, and although he moved boxes and rummaged through a pile of jute sacks and cast-aside blankets, he found nothing.

Back in the runway he listened to the night man snoring and went gingerly toward the open door. As he stood in the opening, his nose was assailed by the smell of stale horse sweat and whiskey. His eyes were accustomed to the darkness by now, but the small, windowless room was pitch dark.

He knew where the saddle and harness pegs were, where an untidy pile of saddle blankets partially filled a corner, and where the little battered desk and chair were. The snoring was coming from the direction of the pile of saddle blankets. He advanced toward it on the balls of his feet, and in the interludes of silence between snores he could hear his own heart.

When he was barely able to make out a wizened silhouette covered by several salt-stiff blankets, he leaned down to find the night man's face. The smell of whiskey was much stronger. He eased one foot forward. It collided with something hard that rolled over several times. George sank to one knee exploring for the object with his hands. It was an empty whiskey bottle.

He rose, put the bottle aside, and went still closer to the snoring hostler. A large rat flashed into sight from among the blankets; George saw it because it was lighter gray than the gloom and because it was moving very fast. It evidently had seen George at very close range, because in its frantic flight it fled directly across the sleeping man's face, digging in with sharp toenails. The snoring broke off abruptly, to be followed by a searing cough as the night man awakened, swinging wildly with both hands.

George stopped breathing.

The old man sat straight up, still striking out blindly. He gasped and wheezed as he twisted toward the doorway — and saw the man's silhouette between it and himself. He seemed to choke for a second or two; then he tried to

150

scream as he kicked and flailed to get clear of the blankets and leap to his feet. In the darkness he was close enough to see a pair of eyes looking down at him from a contorted face with a mouth either badly swollen or badly disfigured — a terrifying caricature of a human face.

He fled past George with his mouth open and his eyes bulging. Because he had been sleeping fully clothed and wearing boots, he made a slight noise as he ran past George toward the rear opening and the alley beyond.

For ten seconds George did not move. The night man did not return, neither was he likely to until full daylight, and by then he would have sworn never to touch whiskey again as long as he lived.

Searching the littered, smelly harness room took time. There were two large boxes nailed to the east wall, which held medicine and brushes but little else. The pile of saddle blankets yielded nothing either. Near the door, where rotting harness had been thrown for years, it was impossible to make a silent search. Most of the harness had chain traces. It rattled each time George searched down through the pile.

He looked inside the little desk and behind it. He even peered inside the small potbellied cast iron heating stove. When he had searched the entire room he returned to the runway, half expecting to see the night man out there. All he saw was that one horse that had been interested in his presence from the time he had walked up the runway.

There was a pole with slats nailed across it that served as the loft ladder. Someone had neglected to close the loft, so he was able to climb up into even greater darkness, but at least the hay was sweetly fragrant. There were two small square doors, one at each end of the loft. He climbed over piles of hay to open the one which was above the rear alley. A little light entered. Evidently there had been a break in the cloud cover, because now he was able to see better.

Using a three-tined hayfork he prodded piles of hay, bumping his head on a Jackson fork which was suspended from ropes above.

Starting at the pile nearest the loft opening, he worked his way slowly toward the rear of the barn, where the mounds of hay were thicker and higher. Whoever did the feeding did it from the piles of hay up front by the loft opening.

He was beginning to believe he would fail again when the tines of his fork struck something solid. By forking hay left and right, he uncovered a gray box. He climbed through the hay to it, lifted it without much effort, and carried it near the rear loft opening, where pale moonlight shone.

The box had a large brass padlock through its hasps. For a moment George knelt without moving. To break the lock would make enough noise to rouse half the town. He tossed the fork away and carried the box to the hole leading down to the runway. It barely passed through, and it was awkward climbing down the pole while balancing the box, but he made it to the ground. Without pausing to catch his breath, he hoisted the box to his shoulder and went out into the alley.

There was not a sound, not even any curious dogs to put his nerves on edge. He carried the box up to the rear of Homer's place, putting it down long enough to open the shed out back. Then he went inside and placed the box on Homer's long unused workbench.

The problem of the big brass padlock solved itself when George leaned down to look closely at it. Beside him was a very heavy crowbar, the kind used by railroad crews when they were laying ties and jockeying rails into place. It fit inside the loop of the lock. George gradually built up the physical pressure as he brought the bar almost down to his knees. He rested, then forced all his weight downward.

The lock broke open without making enough

noise to reach the house. George put the crowbar aside, wiped the sweat off his forehead with his cuff, and raised the lid, perfectly willing to believe he had failed again.

There was a folded brown army blanket inside the box. But beneath it was a crushed sombrero, of the kind vaqueros wore. Below that was a sweat-stained faded blue shirt, a short vaquero jacket, and a pair of tight trousers of either doeskin or goatskin, which had been used enough for the inside of each leg to be shiny from rubbing saddles.

George sought something to sit on, found an empty horseshoe keg, and sank down, feeling more exhausted than if he had run five miles on foot.

Finally, a dog began to bark furiously over on the east side of town. It probably had not picked up George's scent, because the distance was too great and there was no air stirring. But whatever had roused it, perhaps a prowling skunk or raccoon or chicken-roost-hunting coyote, it brought other dogs to full voice throughout town.

George stood up, put the clothing back into the box, shoved it under the flap of a useless buggy top Homer had kept for some reason, and returned to the yard.

There was no latch to the shed door. He had

to improvise one from a stick punched through the mating halves of the old latch. The dogs were still raising Cain when he entered the house from out back, removed his boots and carried them to his room.

Clouds were obscuring the sky again, and he undressed in pitch darkness and crawled into bed. He finally felt very tired. What he had found could be the answer to his riddle, but since vaquero attire was commonplace and could have been stored inside a shock of hay in the loft for some innocent reason, the possibility of its having been used by that mean-looking livery barn hostler during the attempt to kill Maria Antonia would only be valid if either Carter Alvarado or his remudero could identify it as having been worn by the man they had seen with the Winchester rifle.

He closed his eyes, and although he slept, it was a troubled sleep, and he awakened several times before the chill of predawn warned him that if he intended to leave Lordsville without being seen the best time to do so would be within the next hour or so.

He was hungry, which was a fair indication that his stomach had recovered from being battered, but after dressing and going to the kitchen for food, he had difficulty getting it past his swollen, very sore lips.

He filled one pocket with the food he could not eat, hitched Homer's old six-gun around from in front to rest against his right hip, buttoned his coat against the cold, and went back down to the livery barn, almost certain the night man would have recovered from his terror. But the place was just as George had left it. He saddled the sorrel and led it back up the alley. At the shed, he rolled the vaquero attire into a bundle and lashed it, even the huge hat, behind the cantle. He led the animal back to the center of the alley, swung up, and reined northward.

Of one thing he was quite certain. He would have a long wait before Alvarado and his remudero appeared – if they appeared – but there was a slight consolation; northward a few miles there were bosques of trees where a tired man could rest after sunlight arrived to warm the land. *If* it arrived – those clouds were still up there.

By breaking scraps of food into very small pieces he was able to get them past his sore mouth. He did this as he let the sorrel slog along on loose reins. Now the darkness which should shortly be brightening toward a new day seemed instead to become even darker.

Those majestic cloud-galleons he had seen a couple of days ago had flattened out until they stretched from horizon to horizon, and they had turned a menacing dark gray. There was no wind. In fact, there was no sound of any kind. The sorrel's shod hooves passing over hardpan were muffled in layers of powdery dust.

George turned up his collar. To the east a very faint sliver of pewter gray firmed up slowly, so slowly that he was several miles north of Lordsville before it formed a backdrop for some very distant low mountains that stood massively thick and ugly upon the rim of his world.

The air smelled of brimstone. The sorrel's mane came erect as airborne electricity increased. George rode, ate, and studied the sky. He had learned his first year in the South Desert country that while it never rained often enough or at the right times, when it did rain, a year's supply could arrive in just one downpour. It cowed towns, washed out roads, cut deep erosion gullies in the lowest places, and caused a millrace of water inches deep to cover the entire area in just a few hours. And the worst possible place for a man and a horse to be was too far from shelter to reach it in time when the sky opened up.

He finished eating and concentrated on watching the easterly flow of country. That was the direction he expected Carter Alvarado to arrive from. He hoped they would meet before the storm broke. It was possible that they would, because more often than not these black clouds built up for hours, sometimes even a day or two, before the bottom dropped out of them.

George hoped this would be one of those times. He had a thick stand of trees in sight less than a mile ahead when the sky paled below its dark overcast. The sun was rising, but it would not be able to shed much light and warmth as it rose because of the lowness of the clouds.

As he headed into timber cover and stiffly dismounted, he glanced back in the direction of Lordsville. If God willed, as the natives would have said, there would be no deluge until after the funeral of Father O'Malley.

CHAPTER 13

THE MEETING

His horse was very careful to keep the reins to one side as he picked grass heads. George had hobbles on the saddle but rarely used them. He and the sorrel had a tacit understanding: the horse would not run away and George would not ride him hard. No professional rangeman would have relied on anything this tenuous, but Dr. George Brunner was not a rangeman.

Warmth came subtly, although the sun had shown only briefly at dawn before becoming obscured by the massive overcast. George finished his scraps of food, felt his swollen face with its stubble of beard, settled comfortably against the trunk of a rough-barked red fir, and waited.

He also dozed. In fact, when he finally picked up the sound of shod hooves they were very close, otherwise he might have dozed until someone roused him.

He twisted to watch. There were three riders. He recognized Alvarado and Walt Barnard. The Mexican would be Alvarado's man. He was dumpy and thick, with a reddish-bronze complexion.

George got to his feet with a twinge of stiffness in the knees. As the riders came up and halted, he nodded at them. Alvarado dismounted slowly. He had probably heard from Walt Barnard of the beating, but he looked shocked at the condition of the doctor's face. The Mexican dismounted last. He was darkly watchful and impassive.

George went to his horse and returned with the vaquero attire, tossed it on the ground in front of Carter Alvarado, and asked if it looked familiar. Alvarado leaned down without answering to examine it. His remudero walked up and held the hat, which he punched back into shape, dropped it, and picked up the short jacket, which had an overlay design on both sleeves and across the back in faded red leather. He held it up and looked at his employer. "These," he said in Spanish, "the man was wearing."

George let his breath out slowly. He told them where he had found the clothing. Walt picked up the trousers and held them against his body. Walt was a tall man. The liveryman was also tall. Walt smiled slightly at Alvarado and tossed the trousers aside. Evidently Carter Alvarado understood the significance of Walt's gesture because he turned toward the short, thick Mexican. "What would you say?" he asked in Spanish. The Mexican shrugged. "It is possible I was wrong, chief." He looked steadily at Dr. Brunner. "You know that these belong to a North American?"

George's reply was less than direct. "I know I found them hidden in a box in the place where the man who probably shot Maria Antonia Lord works, friend. I know if we can talk to this man he will be able to tell us whether he was wearing them."

George switched to English. He looked at Walt Barnard. "Someone in town could tell us if the hostler was in town the morning of the shooting."

Walt was a direct individual and said outright, "We'd be wasting time." He faced his employer. "They will all be out at the mission this morning."

Carter Alvarado nodded curtly.

Walt's blue eyes did not waver. "Maybe the rifleman will miss his vaquero outfit. If he does, he'll tell whoever his friends are, and they will worry. Or even worse, if he doesn't miss it — if they don't think it's necessary this time — there would be no better time for him to ride out to the Lord place and finish what he started. From what a lady told me last night, the whole countryside mourns the priest. Everyone will be at his funeral."

Carter Alvarado's black eyes widened with understanding. George's eyes did just the opposite, they narrowed to slits. The longer he considered Walt Barnard's innuendo, the more he was disgusted with himself for not having thought the same thing. This would be an ideal opportunity for someone to ride out to the Lord ranch, and although there would certainly be some people out there, most would be in town at the mission for Father O'Malley's funeral. Maria Antonia would be out there; George had told her not to leave her bed. If the killer used simple, basic precaution he could come up to the big house from the east. That would shield him from being detected as he approached. But even if a few women, children, or old people saw him, he could enter the patio, push his way inside the house, and shoot the woman in bed; even the blast of his gun would not carry very far beyond the three-foot-thick walls. Then he could leave as he had arrived, using the big house to screen his escape.

George's weariness vanished. He turned to go after the sorrel horse. Alvarado said something in Spanish to the Mexican. The two of them remained on foot but Walt Barnard swung up over leather, watching Dr. Brunner. Alvarado looked upward. "Don't ride together," he said. "Ride apart. You will see him coming back. I will go to town and wait at the jailhouse." Whoever the killer was, he was in cahoots with Marshal Kandelin. Alvarado turned toward the Mexican. "Go fast to the yard. Find all the riders and bring them swiftly to town with their weapons." The remudero bobbed his head as he was swinging toward his saddle animals.

Walt started reining around as George returned astride. He was pushing the heavy old six-gun back where it belonged as he came up to Carter Alvarado. The rancher told him that he should ride to the Lord place with Walt, and that Chalo, the remudero, would go after the Alvarado riders and bring them to town. He smiled thinly at Dr. Brunner. "I think you and Walt will meet the killer on his way back. Remember that he is a very good shot."

George considered the handsome man. "Coming back?"

Alvarado shrugged. "If you left early, amigo, you can bet he did too. You can't catch him — but you can meet him afterwards. Good luck."

Walt growled at George and led off in a swift lope.

George's mind was unable to think beyond Carter Alvarado's practical words. They could not reach the yard in time to prevent the murder, but they would meet the murderer on his ride back toward town!

He loped beside Walt Barnard staring southwest, the direction of the yard toward which they were angling. Walt looked over once or twice but said nothing until it was time to check up the horses and let them walk for a while.

There was no sun glare and there was no heat. Visibility was better than it could have been if there had been sunshine. George had to curb a desire to force the sorrel horse to run. He had been told the sorrel was not in good physical condition, which was true, although George had been taking him out lately. But stamina in a horse was not the result of desultory exercise, and he knew it.

Walt's horse had one of those artistic and spidery Spanish brands on the left shoulder. The horse was taller and thicker than George's, young and clearly in excellent condition.

George's feeling of helplessness increased when a thin shaft of sunlight penetrated the overcast like a dagger, to touch the ground a mile or two ahead.

They loped again, with Walt keeping an eye on the sorrel horse. He said very little as they put miles behind them. Once, when they surprised a band of Lord loose stock grazing peacefully over the bottom of a fairly deep and very wide swale, Walt watched the surprised horses flee like the wind, laughing as he said, "You know what's prettier than a dancing girl? A running horse in full motion. Look at them."

George was studying the more southerly country. They should be seeing trees and rooftops before long. Walt glanced around, read Brunner's expression correctly, and without speaking pushed the horses a little harder for a mile, by which time they could make out the trees but not the rooftops. Now Walt hauled down to a walk and gestured with a gloved hand. "I'll go south. You stay up here. Maybe he hasn't started back yet; at any rate, there's no sign of him. No sign of any rider. My guess is that he ain't started back yet. We made pretty good time. Doctor, can you use that old gun?"

George, who had been annoyed by the weight and awkwardness of the belt, holster, and weapon, looked briefly downward. "I suppose so."

Walt held out a hand. George passed Homer's Colt to him, and Walt looped his reins to examine the gun. "This thing was made about the same year I was born," he said. He opened the gate and revolved the cylinder. The gun was loaded but the brass casings were green. Walt systematically punched out every load and recharged the weapon from his own shell belt. He handed the gun back with a wag of his head. "George, if this feller's got his rifle along, don't try to shoot it out with him with that gun."

Walt brushed the upthrust butt of his booted carbine. "Even this is no match for a rifle. George, we can't let him stop and get off his horse. If he looks like he's tryin' to do that, aim at the ground in front of his horse. You understand? A carbine is bad enough to shoot from a moving horse, but a long-barreled rifle is worse, and because this gent's one hell of a good shot, we can't let him have any advantage."

George was half listening. He was peering intently in the direction of the yard, with its scattering of buildings. He saw no rider. In fact, he did not see anyone at all, not even when they were less than two miles out with excellent visibility. His heart sank. If Alvarado's estimate was correct, the killing had probably been accomplished, and the killer had eluded them by starting back toward town even before they got down this far.

He was not conscious of sitting rigidly in the saddle until Walt said dryly, "Set easy, will you? It don't help to have your guts in a knot." Walt was prepared to say more, but George raised his right hand and said, "There!"

It wasn't a rider, it was a man and a saddle animal. He was on the east side of the weathered white-washed patio wall. What had caught George's attention was movement; the man had made his horse fast to an exposed log in the rear of the adobe wall and the horse was fidgeting.

Walt sighed. They should have been far apart. As it was, they still had ground for maneuvering, but the distant man behind the white wall would certainly see them before long. Walt made a little hand gesture. "I'm going south. You keep ridin' the way you are. Now remember, if that's him, he's got a rifle that can hit a target a hell of a long distance off."

Walt reined gently to his left and without urging his horse out of its fast walk widened the distance between them.

George was watching the man, whose figure stood out starkly against the whiteness of the mud wall. He had his back to them bending over something. Whatever he was doing held his full attention. He did not even raise his head when some dogs barked among the scattered jacals to the west. It would not have helped even if he had straightened up, because the east section of the patio wall was taller than he was. The dogs continued to bark; they were not barking at the man they could not see, they were barking at Walt and George, the only moving objects in their line of sight over eastward of the hacienda.

George shook sweat off his chin. It was not hot, but his perspiration had nothing to do with the temperature; he had just seen why the man over against the wall had been busy. As he straightened up he was holding a long-barreled rifle in one hand. Evidently he had ridden out here with the weapon disassembled for easier carrying.

George looked for Walt, who was roughly a mile southward. As George watched, Walt turned at a dead walk, riding in the direction of the south side of the big house, and the rifleman saw him. George saw the rifleman stand like stone, watching Walt take a course which could lead him below the main house and perhaps even on around it.

If, George thought, Walt had been wearing vaquero attire, the rifleman might have reacted differently to his presence. But Walt was not dressed as a vaquero and the rifleman was staring very intently at him.

For George, who had not been seen yet, there appeared to be a chance that he could get past the rifleman, down among the trees and into the yard among the outbuildings. He had a fair amount of ground to cover, though, and riding at a walk dragged out the agony to its ultimate degree. He was as tightly wound as a spring, alternately watching the rifleman and the big old shaggy trees, where shadows lay in dark profusion.

Walt may have understood the situation. He continued to walk his horse in the direction of the lower side of the big house, holding the rifleman's attention. Once or twice he stood in his stirrups, shading his eyes with a gloved hand as he peered along the south side of the house, or at something beyond it, over in the direction of the jacals. Not once did he turn his head in the direction of the rifleman.

Even with as much distance separating them as there was, George saw everything Walt did very distinctly. Another time he might have appreciated what had to be Walt's ruse to keep the rifleman's attention on himself and away from George.

The rifleman was tall, easily as tall as Walt. He was holding the rifle across his body with both hands. To throw it to his shoulder for aiming would take brief moments. George had to shake off more sweat.

Walt, easing back down from standing in his stirrups, called loudly and waved in the direction of the back of the house. George could not make out the words but the action had presented him with his last chance to reach the trees. The rifleman's attention was fixed on Walt with fresh concentration, and George rode in among the huge old shaggy trees without having been seen by the rifleman.

He swung to the ground, tugging the sorrel deeper into the shadows. Homer's damn old gun had worked its way around in front again to impede his stride. Irritably, he yanked it to the right and finally got his horse completely hidden among the trees.

He was shaking like a leaf. The horse was perfectly calm, and as he tied it by the reins it began nuzzling the lowest tree limbs, looking for buds or tender shoots.

George could no longer see around the patio to the east side, where the rifleman was, but he had a clear sighting from his place of camouflage to the front gate of the patio. There was nothing to interfere with his crossing the yard to the gate — unless of course the rifleman had the same idea in mind and appeared from

170

around the corner of the wall.

Those barking dogs were still at it, but with less enthusiasm now. There were several small, thick-walled adobe buildings George could use as shelter until the open yard appeared. Then he would be fully exposed for fifty yards or more before reaching the patio gate.

He started forward, using shade and untrimmed low limbs to conceal his passage. There was no sign of the rifleman, or Walt Barnard, or for that matter anyone at all. Except for some desultory barking among the distant mud hutments, the yard was empty and quiet.

He stopped twice, once to look back where the sorrel horse had broken off a low limb making a sharp cracking sound, and for a second time when he was nearing the last of the adobe sheds. At the last stop he shook off sweat and studied the unobstructed yard that had to be crossed before he could get to the patio. While standing motionless to listen and look he thought of Alvarado's words, and spat cotton. Evidently the rifleman had not left town as early as George had, otherwise Alvarado's prediction of a murder already having been committed would have been true.

It was something to be thankful for, but right at this moment George had something else on his mind. By now the killer would have lost sight of Walt Barnard, who would have progressed out of his sight along the south side of the large house, and that meant the killer would be concentrating on something else — his reason for being out here under a leaden and threatening sky while everyone else who could ride or drive was among the mourners at the old mission.

CHAPTER 14

TIME TO BE AFRAID

The trouble with George's second-guessing was that he lacked experience with killers, had no idea how they acted and thought.

The man George was afraid might come around the patio wall the same time he did was not interested in George, because he had not seen him. He was interested in Walt. Instead of coming around the corner of the east wall, the rifleman was stealthily walking in the opposite direction, in an effort to keep Walt in sight.

George stood and sweated, scanning the area for some sign of a man with a rifle. When none appeared, he took a big breath and started walking. As he left cover he pulled out Homer's six-gun and let it hang at his side, his thumb on the hammer for instant cocking.

He was not a good shot with a pistol — he

was not a good shot with a rifle either. He had fired guns but had never cared enough about them to practice. He was acutely aware of this — and of the marksmanship of his adversary — as he continued briskly up to the patio gate, paused to listen, and pushed on inside. He was now surrounded by the three adobe patio walls. The fourth wall was the front of the house. His entire perspective, which had been practically unlimited up to this moment, was abruptly shortened on all sides to a matter of a few yards.

He did not feel sheltered, he felt instead highly vulnerable. His palm was slippery around the gunstock as he looked in all directions before proceeding to the steel-studded old oaken door. Now even the dogs were silent. There was one sound, softly distant; the cry of a mourning dove.

He tried the old iron latch; it worked perfectly. Under his squeezing fingers it raised the *tranca* on the inside and the door began to open inward of its own weight. Faint fragrance and coolness came up to him as he raised the old gun and entered, leaning against the door to close it.

No one appeared, and at this moment he would have welcomed even the squatty girl with the ribbons in her hair.

The moment the door closed he could no

longer hear the mourning dove, which was just as well, because it did not make a very reassuring call.

His heart was pounding. He stood with his back to the door for a moment, breathing deeply, listening for sounds of people. He had never been beyond the parlor, a hallway, and one bedroom; he had no idea how many people were required to maintain the Lord hacienda, but he did know that there were servants, because when he had needed basins of water and towels they had brought them. Now no one appeared and there were no sounds coming from any of the other rooms. Doña Teresa Maria, who in the past had seemed to have an almost uncanny knack of knowing when he was at the front door, would almost certainly be ten miles away at Father O'Malley's funeral. But until it occurred to him that he had not knocked on the door to alert servants that there was a visitor, the utter stillness unnerved him.

Shifting the gun to his left hand, he dried his right palm down a trouser leg, gripped the weapon again, and crossed the large parlor, with its sparse, massively heavy and hand carved furniture.

He had just one advantage. No one, including the rifleman, knew he was here, but at any second he could lose that advantage.

The domed hallway was heavily shadowed, as it always had been, because for its full length there were no windows. Instead there was a series of closed doors. Here the fragrance yielded to a more familiar and less appealing scent — carbolic acid.

He was careful to glide over the hallway's red tiles as soundlessly as possible, coming at last to the door of Maria Antonia's bedroom. He reached for the iron latch. Another time he would have rapped discreetly; today it did not occur to him to do this. He squeezed, heard a faint whisper of sound as the small bar inside rose from its hangers, and pushed the door gently inward.

He half expected the bed to be empty. It wasn't, but Maria Antonia was sleeping, her breathing faintly audible as a soft sweep of whispery sound.

He eased the door closed and leaned back against it, looking at the beautiful woman. He had to fumble several times before he managed to holster the gun; then he pushed the weight of gun and leather to the right and leaned on the door again, waiting for his heartbeat to settle down.

In this place of timeless serenity he actually began to have a sensation of safe sanctuary, but it never got beyond its beginning. Whatever had delayed the killer would not last. The man was here to do his work as quickly as he could and escape.

As George was straightening up off the door it crossed his mind that he had helped the killer; he had not dropped the steel pin above the tranca from inside the front door to lock it. For a moment he considered returning to the parlor, but Maria Antonia's head rolled gently on the low pillow, her eyes open and continuing to widen as she stared speechlessly at him.

He knew how he looked — rumpled, sweaty, unshaven, red-faced, with a grotesquely twisted and swollen mouth, and with a gun hanging on his right hip.

He said, "The man who shot you is back." At the expression this statement caused, he went forward, and leaning on the back of a chair, he told her that he and Walt Barnard had come out here to prevent her murder. The more he talked, the paler she got. When he had said all that was necessary she neither looked away nor blinked. She seemed too stunned to do either.

He remembered his earlier error and went back to the bedroom door to drop the locking pin into place, then returned to the chair and sank down onto it, looking at her. He tried to smile. Even if he had been clean-shaven, it would not have been a success. His disfigured lower face made the smile a grimace.

She finally spoke. "He is — here? In the yard?"

"I'm not sure where he is. We saw him putting his rifle together on the east side of the patio."

"You are sure?"

"Yes. Carter Alvarado is in Lordsville. By now I suppose his vaqueros have gotten down there too."

The large black eyes were utterly still. "In Lordsville? He wouldn't come out here?"

"Maria, it's not just the man with the rifle. There are other men involved. One of them is Marshal Kandelin." George raised his hand. "He waylaid me yesterday on my way back to town from out here. This is his handiwork. Mr. Alvarado is going to keep anything else from happening in town until Walt Barnard and I get back with the killer."

She finally shifted slightly under the blanket, raised a hand to grope beneath her low pillow, and withdrew the hand holding a nickel-plated, under-and-over .41 caliber pistol with a two-inch barrel. George eyed the little gun with more skepticism than curiosity. He had seen these weapons before, and although he had neither owned nor fired one, he had never heard anyone say their accuracy was much greater than the width of a room — and they held only two bullets.

She said, "George, is he inside the house?"

He offered a delayed response, thinking again of his oversight with the front door. "I don't know. I don't think he is or by now he would be trying to shoot your bedroom door open."

"Who is he?"

"A hostler who works at the livery barn in town. I'm sure I've heard his name, but right now I can't remember it."

She put the hand with the little gun in it atop the blanket. "A fairly large man with dark eyes and a cruel mouth?"

George thought that was a fair description and nodded his head.

"His name is Henry Stoll. He worked for my father six or seven years ago. Juan Esteven caught him inside this house once when we were away. He was going through the drawers, and he had opened my father's safe. After he was fired, I met him one afternoon on the range. He told me he would get even with us if it was the last thing he ever did. . . . Remember when you asked me for names? I thought of him."

"Why didn't you tell me?"

"My father said he was a sneak thief, and that a man like that might make threats but he was the least likely of all men to make good on them."

George looked at the beautiful woman. Her father had been very wrong. Such a misjudgment of character normally would not matter, except that right now Henry Stoll was coming to commit murder.

He rose and crossed to the closed window. Beyond, Lord's Land ran for miles, clearly visible and with nothing moving out there. The overcast seemed not to have lowered any. He pulled the drapes across the barred window, which immediately made the room very dark, and lit two candles, leaving them on their silver plates atop her dresser.

He went to the door to listen. There was not a sound. That worried him more than it reassured him. If he could know where Walt Barnard was . . . The last he had seen of him, Walt had been diverting the rifleman's attention down toward the south side of the house.

He returned to the bedside chair but did not sit down. Maria Antonia motioned toward a basin atop the small marble-topped table. "It will help your face," she said. "The water is cold."

He nodded absently. He was thinking that this was probably how a condemned man felt while he was waiting to be hanged. She continued to watch him. After a while she said, "Why doesn't he come? There is no one in the house to stop him. There will be no one until late this evening when they return from the funeral."

Dr. Brunner gave her a gargoyle grin. "The people among the jacals?"

She faintly shook her head. "Esteven led most of them to the mission before dawn this morning. But even if there were some of the men over there, how would they know what is going on here?"

He paced to the door to listen again. He dreaded the showdown, but he thought he dreaded the waiting and the uncertainty even more.

What he particularly wondered about was Walt Barnard. Possibly he and the man named Henry Stoll were playing a deadly game of stalking each other. If that was not it, he could not imagine what was happening outside the house.

He finally decided to go back through the parlor and bolt the front door, but as he raised his hand to remove the pin from the bedroom door Maria Antonia said, "George — if you go out there, that may be exactly what he is waiting for."

George did not think so. "He didn't see me, Maria. He doesn't know I'm here, let alone in the house. He was watching Walt. That gave me time to get into the yard out of sight."

George reached to lift the bolt as a muted but unmistakable gunshot sounded from beyond the house somewhere. He left the bolt in place and turned back toward the bed. Maria Antonia's large dark eyes were fixed on him. "Don't go," she whispered. "Help me sit up."

He scowled at her. "Lie still."

"But I can sit up. I did it yesterday and I've done it today."

A tremendous crash of thunder blew the stillness apart for fifty miles in all directions. Its growly aftermath continued to rumble for a full two minutes after the initial sound.

Maria put both hands to her mouth. The little gun was lying forgotten atop the covers. The candles wavered, making the soft light move eerily and unsteadily from wall to wall.

George finally went to the marble-topped table, but to fill a drinking glass from a pitcher, not to cool his face in the basin. He drank two glasses of water and offered Maria Antonia a glass. She shook her head, still with her hands over her mouth. When the last echo died she lowered her hands. "I'm afraid of thunder," she said.

He nodded. It had not frightened him as much as it had unsettled him. Normally thunder had no effect on him at all, but this was not a normal circumstance — waiting in a feebly lit room deep inside a fortresslike adobe house for a killer to appear.

He drank a third glass of water and offered another rueful smile. "Whiskey would be better, and I don't really like it."

"George, where is your friend?"

"I wish I knew. When I was a youngster my father took me hunting a lot. One time when we heard a lot of gunfire he told me that a fusillade usually meant a hunter had missed his first shot and was trying to make up for it by blazing away. He said when you only heard one shot, and afterward nothing but silence, it probably meant that the hunter had brought something down. . . . That gunshot we heard before the thunder . . . I wish I knew where Walt was."

Maria Antonia picked up the small gun again and held it atop the bedding. "George?"

"Yes."

"My aunt is afraid of you."

He blinked at her. "Afraid? Why? I can't imagine having done anything to make her feel that way."

"She — haven't you noticed how she watches us when you are out here?"

"Yes. She's worried about you. My impression is that she is very protective of you." As he finished speaking he remembered something Juan Esteven had casually said, and stared at her.

"She is protective. She is a childless widow and I am her only living relation. She – the reason she is . . . the reason she watches us like an eagle is because I told her I am very fond of you."

He stood as though he had become rooted.

There was another faintly-heard gunshot, but this time the sound was different. The first shot had sounded sharp, high-pitched. This second shot made a deeper sound, more like the roar of a muffled cannon. He knew that sound. It had been made by someone's six-shooter.

CHAPTER 15

A SMALL, EMPTY GUN

Not knowing was worse than the waiting. He went restlessly back to the window, parted the drapes, and looked out, and because his eyes had become accustomed to the light of the room, even cloudy daylight beyond the window made him squint.

There still was nothing out there, but he heard dogs barking again as he let the drape fall back into place and turned to face the bed. He had never envisioned himself as a hero and he still did not, but he was worried about Walt and wished he could leave Maria Antonia alone long enough to return to the yard.

She asked for water. He got her a glass and stood beside the bed as she drank, then took back the glass. Their eyes met and held. Since entering the house he had felt resigned. He still felt that way; fearful and fatalistically resigned. If Henry Stoll burst into the room he would kill them both.

Maria Antonia smiled up at him. "I am grateful to you and your friend. I don't know him — maybe he's in his element. But you are a doctor, not a gunfighter."

He would never argue that issue with her, but instead of agreeing he said, "I want to tell you something I have no right to say — except that unless I say it now I may never be able to say it. You are the most beautiful woman I have ever seen."

He turned away and went to the door to listen. Her eyes followed him. As he straightened up a small sound reached him through the door. It was not repeated, so he could not be sure, but it had sounded like footsteps in the tiled hallway. He held his breath, hearing his heartbeat again, and very gently stepped away from the door.

Behind him, Maria Antonia's color faded. She gripped the little gun without raising it. She had heard nothing, but George's obvious alertness was enough. She whispered, "What is it?"

He half turned and held a finger to his mouth, then faced the door again. Since he had closed the drapes and had lit the brace of candles, time had seemed to stop. There was no longer any indication of its passing. The light, the semi-darkness, the utter quiet, seemed to blend in a period of eerie stillness without a significant passing of time.

Beyond, out in the domed hallway, a probing hand examined the door and stopped moving near the latch. George had to dry sweat from his right palm again before lifting Homer's gun from its holster. Behind him, Maria Antonia lay still in the faint candlelight, her knuckles white from gripping the little gun.

There was not a shred of doubt in George's mind about the identity of the man beyond the oaken door. If it had been Walt, he would have called out.

If it was anyone else, a servant, someone from the jacals, he would not have explored the door, he would have knocked on it.

George had sweat running beneath his shirt. There were three people in the house, a beautiful woman whose helplessness went beyond being bedridden, a physician who was holding a gun but who had not fired one in something like fifteen years, and a deadly killer who had somehow got past Walt and was now prepared to do what he had ridden out here to do: commit murder.

George had no illusions. He thought of firing

through the door, but every door he had seen in this house was made of oak, doubled and steel reinforced. The wood was old; it had cured to the density of light steel. Even at close range a handgun slug would not penetrate it.

He derived no satisfaction from the fact that this worked both ways; if he could not fire *out* through the door, Stoll could not fire *in* through the door. But Stoll could certainly blow off the latch, and that, George told himself, was why he had been exploring the door with his hand. He was seeking its weakest point.

Finally, the closeness of the room became noticeable. When the window and drapes had been open, there had been fresh air. Now, with the candles consuming oxygen and replacing it with their faint odor of animal fat and wax, the air smelled stale.

Stoll stopped testing the door. George guessed that the deafening gunshot that smashed the latch would come next. He glanced once toward the bed, then raised Homer's gun, cocked it, and waited, perspiration running past his lips with a salty taste.

He stood at the left of the door, which was hinged to swing inward from the right. George moved slightly toward the little table with the marble top so that when the door was blown open he would be clear of it.

Seconds passed with unprecedented slowness. Stoll seemed almost to be deliberately delaying his final assault. But George did not believe this. Stoll had to commit his murder — now two murders — and get away swiftly.

But the stunning gunshot did not come. George flashed another quick look at Maria Antonia. Pale though she was, her jaw was set, her black eyes were on the door, and she held the gun pointing directly at the door. He could almost see her dead father in the determined expression on her face. Like Davy Crockett at the Alamo, she might die in bed, but she would do it showing defiance to the last breath.

In the hallway a man's booted feet sounded faintly as he stepped away. He seemed to be moving to his left, so as not to be in a direct line with the latch when he blew it apart.

George dried his palm one more time, cocked Homer's six-gun, and raised it.

The muzzle blast was thunderous, even through the oak door. On the inside of the room the pin preventing the tranca from rising, tore free of its leather thong and flew upward like a small projectile, striking the ceiling and dropping back to the floor. The latch and tranca were driven into the wood, completely shattered, but while the bullet at close range had smashed the latch, it had not done so until the door had absorbed the full force of the blast, so the door did not swing open. It was hanging loose, though. Anyone had only to gently push from the outside to make it swing inward.

Black-powder gunsmoke added a bitter scent to the stale air, but with it came a rush of fresh air from the hallway. George watched one candle flicker wildly and succumb. The remaining candle flame twisted and guttered but did not die. Now the room was even darker.

For a long time the echo of the gunshot bounced from wall to wall without diminishing, and when it finally ended George's ears were still ringing. He steadied the aimed, cocked six-gun, expecting another shot to blow the door open before Henry Stoll sprang inside to kill what he probably was confident would be a helpless woman.

George made his misjudgment from ignorance. Stoll did not push the door for a long time, and when he finally did, there was no sign of him. Neither was there any sound from where he was standing in the hallway. Men who were not novices at this kind of murder did not spring wildly through a doorway, gun blazing. George was picking up knowledge minute by minute. It was the kind of learning a man would probably never have to rely on again in his lifetime, especially if his trade had nothing at all to do with guns and gunmen.

Stoll was a cautious but knowledgeable killer. He rolled his hat into the darkened room. George squeezed the trigger before he realized the purpose of Stroll's ruse. He stopped squeezing. The only thing that prevented Homer's gun from firing, which would have told Stoll that Maria Antonia was not alone, was the fact that it still had the original trigger spring. (Almost invariably men who bought those guns new took them to gunsmiths to have the trigger pull corrected so that the guns fired at a very slight pressure. Homer had never done this.)

George saw Maria Antonia from the corner of his eyes. She had not even aimed at the hat. She was staring intently into the empty hallway.

The waiting began again. Henry Stoll had to decide whether the ruse had failed because the woman in the bed had not seen the hat, or because she had no weapon.

George heard him come up onto the toes of his boots. Stoll had made his decision. But he still did not jump through the doorway; instead he jumped past it to the opposite side. George saw only a flash of movement. He knew where

191

the killer was, on the west side of the doorway. George took two soundless steps to fade from sight behind the door.

Stoll gave an icy chuckle from the hallway. "Lady, why didn't you fire? I seen that little gun. . . . Lady, I'm goin' to jump past the doorway again—take a shot."

George wigwagged his gun to attract Maria Antonia's attention. She darted a look at him and he vigorously nodded his head. She raised the gun, waited for Stoll to flash past again, and fired.

She missed. The large caliber slug tore a handsized chunk out of the whitewashed adobe wall on the far side of the hallway, but most noticeable was the deafening sound. She had fired from inside her room; the reverberation had nowhere to go.

Stoll laughed, heartily this time. "Lady, you couldn't hit the broad side of a barn from the inside. . . . You ready?" He flashed past one more time, and George watched Maria Antonia. She did not squeeze the trigger until Stoll was already past her sight.

George thought he understood why she had done that. He felt the full burden of their defense resting on him now, and he gritted his teeth, holding the six-gun ready.

Stoll laughed again. "All right, señorita —

you had two slugs and you fired two slugs." He appeared around the left-hand edge doorsill. He was holding a six-gun at his side, looking through the semi-darkness at her. His teeth shone, as did the mean, merciless expression when he smiled.

He said, "I told you I'd get even. I'd have done it that day at the cemetery if the damn sun hadn't been so bright. The range was a mite long, too. Not like now."

Henry Stoll stepped into the room. He and Maria Antonia looked steadily at one another. George knew where Stoll was but could not see him until the man moved closer to the bed, still letting the six-gun hang at his side. He clearly wanted to prolong Maria Antonia's terror. If he had turned his head only a couple of inches, he would have been able to discern the dark silhouette, the gun pointed at him. Instead Stoll concentrated on the beautiful woman in the bed, whose black eyes were huge in her white face.

"Lady, you're likely goin' to meet that preacher who died. The one they're havin' the big funeral for today. He sure died at a good time. Everyone'll be out there wailin' and wearin' black. In here it's just you an' me, ain't it?"

Maria Antonia spoke in a faintly breathless

tone of voice. "Why? Just because my father fired you? That's no reason to kill someone."

Stoll continued to smile wolfishly. "No, it ain't, Lady. But you see, there's four of us who are goin' to bid in your ranch when there ain't no more heirs. That's why."

Stoll stopped smiling and began to raise his gun. George said, "You bastard," and pulled the trigger. This time Homer's gun went off. The explosion was blinding and deafening. Stoll bawled and fought hard to stay on his feet. George had no idea where the bullet had hit the man, but he saw Stoll grab a bedpost to keep from going down. George was pulling the hammer back for his next shot, but Henry Stoll fired first. His bullet went straight down into the floor, roughly halfway between them. He looked at George in the semidarkness with bulging eyes. His lips moved. The only thing that came out was a trickle of blood. He released his grip on the bedpost and fell.

Maria Antonia had been rigid, scarcely breathing. Now, ears ringing, heart pounding, she eased back a little at a time, feeling along the bed with her hands, and finally dropped back down on the low pillow as still as stone.

George watched her instead of Henry Stoll. He thought she had fainted. He crossed to the foot of the bed, kicked Stoll's six-gun out into the hallway, where it rattled over the tiles, and stepped past to pull aside the drapes and let some of the gunmetal gray daylight into the room.

With much better visibility he shoved Homer's gun into its floppy holster and knelt beside Henry Stoll. Their eyes met, and George recognized the glassy look of shock. He put two fingers against Stoll's neck, picking up a very faint pulse, and leaned down to look closer, inside Stoll's gray jacket. He did not have to search. His bullet had hit the killer high on the left side and had exited even higher on the right side. At the very best, Henry Stoll had only moments. George sat back. Stoll's pupils were darkening. He still lived, but his eyes no longer focused. There was no point in trying to talk to him. George stood up, let go a loud, unsteady breath, and went over to the side of the bed.

Maria Antonia looked at him. "Is he dead?"

"In another minute, no more." He took one of her hands in both of his. "Tell me where the whiskey is. You need some."

"In the kitchen. To your left through the dining room."

He returned with a glass, half full, and handed it to her. "Drink it and try to relax.

Don't look at the floor," he said. "I've got to find Walt."

She said, "I have never been so afraid in my life."

He squeezed her hand. "Neither have I. Drink it slowly. I'll be back as quickly as I can."

She watched him until he was out of her sight around the corner of the doorway; then she listened to his diminishing footfalls. Only when she heard the front door close did she raise the glass to sip whiskey.

CHAPTER 16

ANOTHER PRACTITIONER

There was not a sound in the gray day until George reached the barn. A dog barked and was immediately scolded into silence.

He went down through the barn and stood in the rear opening, gazing in the direction of the jacals. There was not a soul in sight. Lazy spindrifts of smoke rose from mud-wattle chimneys. They went straight up because there was not a breath stirring. The clouds were even lower than they had been an hour earlier. That thunderous roll of widespread sound had presaged the nearness of the eventual downpour. In his two years among the residents of the South Desert he had never before seen a Mexican settlement looking as deserted and empty. Even in times of anxiety there had been dogs, children, scratching chickens, and old mothers and grandfathers moving or sitting in shade. Here there were none of these things, and he almost believed that the houses had been abandoned, except for the thin spindrifts of smoke.

He walked from the corrals behind the barn in the direction of the nearest mud house, halting a few yards away, and called out in Spanish. "Oh-yay, friends! Be at ease. It is I, the doctor. I am looking for my companion—he may be injured. At the house there is a dead man. The lady is safe. I need you to answer me! I am looking for my companion."

He listened to the echoes of his badly accented Spanish and waited. It was a long wait before a stout, short, very dark woman with gray hair appeared in a jacal doorway, hands on her hips. She was evidently a no-nonsense individual. "Where is the one who shot your companion?" she called shortly.

"Señora, I told you. He is dead at the main house."

The burly woman with her granite expression and dark eyes fixed bleakly on George cocked her head, as though listening to someone speaking who was behind her, out of George's vision. She dropped her arms and shifted slightly so she was no longer blocking the doorway. "Your companion is here."

"*Muerte*, señora?"

"No, no, he lives. Come." As she said this the woman leaned out to peer in all directions. "Are there more, Doctor?" she said as George walked forward. "Are you sure the one who lies dead did not have companions who are somewhere close?"

As he reached the doorway he replied, "He was alone, señora. There are others, but they are in Lordsville." She moved clear, but the interior of the jacal was even darker than Maria Antonia's room had been, and he hesitated. A lithe young girl lifted a bucket from a guttering candle and it was instantly revived. Two more buckets were lifted.

The room was fairly large. Religious statues, carved of wood and invariably showing great amounts of blood flowing from the crucified figure, were on every wall, along with religious paintings and pictures from books and newspapers. There were no beds, but there was a beehive oven in one corner, a table, chairs with goat-skin seats, and a number of very black old cooking pots suspended near the oven from thornpin pegs driven into the adobe wall.

There were several people, but the lithe girl was the only young one. The others were as old as the burly woman, or older, and stood like statues, only their eyes moving, following George as he crossed to a pallet of blankets and knelt. Walt looked up at him. His face had a crude, thick bandage covering nearly all of it. Blood had seeped through the cloth.

George considered the bandage, guessed at the nature of the wound, sniffed at an unfamiliar smell coming from the bandage, and said, "Walt . . . ?"

The thick, dark woman immediately spoke. "No, señor, he must not talk. We can tell you. Someone saw him leave his horse carrying a carbine. The horse wandered over to the barn. There was another man hunting for him. He knew it. We all went indoors with the children and dogs, to wait. The other man had a long-barreled gun. This one, he went in beside a house waiting for the other man to walk past. The other man did not walk past, he came in behind your friend. This one dropped flat as the man with the big gun shot at him. The man missed and your friend fired back with his belt gun. He also missed. The rifleman jumped out of sight behind a house. Your friend stood up. For a long time there was nothing, then your friend went looking for the man with the big gun. They were behind a house so we could not see them, but someone fired with a handgun. It was this one. We thought it was over. Moments passed. There was one more shot from a handgun. After that it really was over.

Your friend came crawling from behind the house on all fours, like a goat. There was blood everywhere. The man with the big gun went from there directly over to the big house and went inside the patio. That was when some of us went over to get your companion and bring him here. He was shot through the face." As the unsmiling woman stopped speaking she looked toward Walt's pallet. "They came for me. I cared for his injury," she added.

George looked down again. Walt was looking past him at the dark, barrel-shaped, unsmiling older woman. George turned back too. "Where in the face was he shot, señora?"

"All the way through. From one side to the other, but the bullet hit no teeth. It went from cheek to the other cheek. He is a very lucky man. By now the bleeding will have stopped. The healing will be working. In two weeks he will have two big dimples. In time the scars will get small, but he will always have them."

Someone chuckled. George ignored this. He gazed steadily at the woman. Her very dark eyes had muddy whites. One thing about her was obvious; she was a curandera. No one disputed her knowledge and no one argued with her decisions. She could have been forty or sixty-five.

George said, "The medicine, señora?"

"A very old one, Doctor. It never fails to stop bleeding. There will be then a fever and I will draw it away so there can be no infection."

"You will prevent a fever? How?"

"The way I always have, señor. The way my mother and grandmother always did. First with ice, then before the freezing stops, with the entrails of a chicken to be applied while they are still warm. Three applications, each one tied tightly to the wounds. After that, a poultice of wet clay, so that as it dries and pulls together and turns hard it will close the wounds."

George said no more as he faced around and met Walt's twinkling blue gaze. One thing seemed obvious; Walt was in no particular pain. George nodded his head to convey understanding, if not necessarily approval. He told Walt what had happened in the house — Walt's eyes never left his face. When George finished, Walt raised a hand, and using a stiff forefinger made four distinct letters in the air. G-O-O-D. He paused, then wrote two more words in the air. N-O-W W-H-A-T.

George rose to his feet and shoved Homer's gun back around where it was supposed to be. The damn thing invariably worked its way around to the front and hung heavily where it interfered with the movement of his upper legs.

He had not thought about the aftermath of the shootings. "Wait, I suppose. I could ride back to town, but it's late in the day; Juan Esteven and the others ought to be back from the funeral before long. I don't like the idea of leaving you and Maria Antonia alone."

Walt made no more gestures. George glanced around among the dark faces and ended up looking at the sturdy woman. She looked straight back at him.

She obviously knew who he was—the doctor who had been treating the lady at the big house. She was not defiant, but she was clearly resolute. He may not have been the first medical doctor she had encountered, but regardless of that, there was not a yielding bone in her sturdy body. She had been applying cures for many years and had learned her trade from others who had done the same for even more years. She lost some patients, exactly as the doctor lost some, probably no more and no less.

George went back out under the black sky. Now there was a little wind coming from the northeast. The woman followed him, and when he sniffed the air, she said, "It will rain. Your companion must not get wet."

He could agree with that. It was the business of the insides of chickens and clay he had trouble with. This woman was not the first of her profession he had encountered – it had not done anything for his pride or professionalism to know that some of the people he had treated had subsequently summoned curanderas.

He turned slowly to meet the unwaveringly hard gaze of the older woman. Before he could speak she surprised him. "I know about carbolic acid and ether, about Laudanum and stomach powders," she said in careful, knowledgeable English. "I was sent to a mission school for six years. I use the best of both systems, Doctor."

He was silent for a while. "You kill and split a chicken and tie it over wounds, señora?"

She hung fire for a long moment. "Yes, I know it will draw out infection. I have seen this happen many, many times. Does your carbolic acid do that?"

Before he could answer there was another of those reverberating rolls of thunder. He thought of Maria Antonia, afraid of thunder and alone. He waited until the woman would be able to hear him, then said, "*Pardona mi, señora*. I will come back later."

As he hastened across the yard, she stood watching him, still wearing her unyielding expression. Then she returned to the jacal as the first few scattered raindrops fell, making puffball-like explosions in the dust of the yard.

The front door was open. George passed inside, closed it, and went briskly to the bedroom, where Maria Antonia looked very relieved when she saw him. He only glanced once at Henry Stoll before positioning himself so that he was blocking her view in that direction.

Her face had bright color, the whiskey glass was empty, and it occurred to him that she probably had not eaten since early morning and it was now late afternoon. He told her about Walt and the curandera. She glanced toward the window. "There have always been curanderas, George. There probably always will be." She paused long enough to turn back to face him. "When I was small one of the vaqueros was bitten in the leg by a rattlesnake. He rode four miles to get back to the yard. He had a high fever and was out of his head some of the time. That same woman you met, who cared for your friend, cured him. My father said it was ridiculous, she couldn't do it. He said that immediately after someone is bitten by a rattlesnake the wound has to be opened and the poison sucked out. That wasn't done with the vaquero until he got back to the yard, and then it was too late. But she made a poultice that turned the leg almost black. She changed it every three hours. She sat with the vaquero for two days, until the blackness left and the swelling went down. Two days after that the man could stand up and walk around, but he was too weak to ride again for another two weeks."

George was interested. "What did your father say?"

"That the vaquero was young and strong as an ox." She smiled at him. "Did you know my father?"

"I knew him when I saw him."

"He would admit he was wrong when there was no other course. That time he did not admit it."

The rain was increasing. It brought a chill to the interior of the house. George closed the window, turning to face the doorway when two old Mexicans appeared, hats in hand. They had been sent, they said, to see if they could help. George pointed to the dead man and without a word they carried him out of the room.

George asked Maria Antonia if the chunky girl who wore hair ribbons had gone to the mission. She nodded. "Everyone went, except those elderly people you saw. George, you can have your friend brought here. There are spare rooms."

"No," he said, listening to the increasing sound of heavy rainfall. "He'll be all right where he is, for a while, anyway. Maria, you must be hungry."

She wasn't. "Very tired, but not hungry. Is it time for the others to be back?"

It probably was time but he had seen no sign of them. "Soon, I hope."

"You know where the kitchen is. You look starved."

"And dirty, and unshaven, and tired."

They smiled at each other.

At that moment the curandera and another, even older, woman appeared in the doorway. Both regarded Maria Antonia owlishly. Both also glanced at the floor near the foot of the bed; they had certainly seen the dead gunman and had heard from the men who had carried him down to the barn where they had found him. The older woman said they would light fires and start to prepare a meal. Neither of them awaited a reply but departed in the direction of the kitchen.

George sat down. Maria Antonia watched him—and smiled. "I have been to New York," she told him. "I suppose the look on my face up there was the same as the look on your face now. Everything was so different up there. George?"

He smiled. "One nation, two worlds, Maria." He arose. "Sleep. I'll be back in a while."

She did not ask where he is going, but she watched him leave, then relaxed and closed her eyes.

The fragrance from the kitchen drew him like a magnet. The older woman smiled but the curandera did not seem to know how to smile. It was easy to guess that during her long life she had known hardship. To win her smile would require more than humor.

They fed him at a kitchen table. They also gave him watered whiskey with peppermint in it. He listened to the downpour, took his peppermint whiskey with him to the parlor, and stood near the blazing fire looking out into the patio through the only large window in the entire house. Water came in sheets, perpendicular waves of it, one behind the other sweeping in from the north. Under a tin roof of the kind they had in Lordsville, the sound would have been deafening. Out here it was not that loud, nevertheless it would have been impossible to carry on a conversation.

The fire in the hearth cast a surprising amount of heat. It had long been George Brunner's opinion that wood-stoves were much more efficient than fireplaces. But an open fire on a stormy day fed the soul, something a functional stove could not do. And while this particular fire may have been losing half or two thirds of its heat up the chimney, it still put enough heat out into the large room to make him move away from it.

He sipped from his cup and eyed the blaze. It was intensely hot. The reason for the extraordinary amount of heat was that the wood was not pine or fire, or even cedar, it was old twisted lengths of dry manzanita, gray on the outside and blood red on the inside. He had heard many times that burning dry manzanita in a steel stove, even if its bottom was lined with firebrick, would result in the fierce heat burning the bottom out.

Maybe. In a fireplace it cast forth more heat than any other wood. He went to a very old, hand carved sofa with red cushions and sat down, sipping watered whiskey and listening to the storm, and unconsciously relaxed in every joint as waves of heat passed over and around him.

He put the empty glass aside, settled his scuffed boots over one armrest, punched up a red pillow under his neck and head at the other end of the sofa, and watched the rain out in the patio. And fell asleep.

CHAPTER 17

A DAY LATER

It was a very long, dark, tumultuous night. There was high wind pushing forcefully against the heavy clouds, but it made no impression on the heart of the storm, which was somewhere between Lordsville and the yard of Lord's Land. There was a deluge in that area and for a hundred miles in all directions.

The earth was dry, so a great amount of water was absorbed. Then the earth swelled closed, and with nowhere to go, the water built up throughout the long period of darkness until in the wet grayness of the new day it was like a lake as far as a person could see.

George slept on.

People stirred in the big house. A vaquero brought more wood; the squatty girl who wore ribbons in her hair hovered between the parlor and the kitchen like a mother hen with only one chick.

She bathed George's face in warm water, and he did not even change the cadence of his breathing. Doña Teresa Maria came to stand looking down at him, her stone-set features unchanged. She left, and the curandera approached resolutely with a basin of hot water, which she put upon a small table, and went back to the kitchen for a low stool. She sent the squatty girl for towels and soap. When the girl returned the older woman was holding an ivory-handled straight razor poised above the sleeping man's face. The girl's eyes sprang wide open. She whispered in alarm. "Señora, he will move."

Without so much as glancing around at the girl the older woman spoke in Spanish. "It will be to his sorrow if he does. Bring the lamp from the kitchen table." She did not wait for better light but lathered George's face and swooped low with her razor. When the girl returned she said, "Put it close. Pull over a chair and use that."

The girl watched entranced as the dark hand moved with surprising swift lightness. Clearly, the older woman had done this before, perhaps many times.

Doña Teresa Maria appeared from the domed

hallway, put another manzanita burl into the fire, and came to stand with hands clasped over her flat middle, watching. The curandera ignored them both. Teresa Maria said softly, "Do you know what happened to his face?"

The other woman did not allow her gaze to stray as she answered curtly, "No, señora."

"The marshal of Lordsville beat him senseless." Doña Teresa Maria leaned down slightly. "You treated his mouth?"

"Yes."

"And the swelling is almost gone?"

"Yes, as you can see, señora." The curandera sat back, wiped the blade, and examined her work. She leaned to make three more sweeps, then dropped the razor into the basin and raised her eyes to the squatty girl. "You may wash his face," she said, and rose from the stool. "I have the other one to look out for."

The girl sat on the stool, Teresa Maria's presence making her nervous. The curandera held a poncho above her head and left the house.

Teresa Maria left the parlor. The squatty girl finished with the washing and sat gazing at the sleeping gringo. He opened one eye. She reddened. He opened the other eye and raised a hand to his face. His lips were almost normal again. The places where scabs had been were

212

white and sensitive, but the scabs were gone. He gathered himself to rise and the girl sprang up to move away.

For a full minute George sat forward on the edge of the red cushions, then began turning his head from side to side. His neck was slightly stiff; otherwise he felt better today than he had felt at any time yesterday. He smiled at the girl and she colored again as she smiled back. "There is a meal in the kitchen for you," she said.

George nodded and rocked his head so far back he did not see Teresa Maria come up, expressionless as always, erect, directly gazing at him. The girl took the basin and fled.

He brought his head forward, met the older woman's very dark eyes, and sighed. "You must have gotten wet last night," he said in English.

She answered shortly, "Yes, we got wet, but the rain did not become bad until we were less than a mile out. . . . Doctor?"

"Yes'm."

"There is hot water in the tub for you to bathe."

He nodded. "I'm grateful, señora. First, though, I want to see my friend."

Her very dark eyebrows rose slightly. "Not my niece, Doctor?"

He shoved himself to his feet. The couch had

not been designed for use as a bed. His legs ached, his neck also ached, and his back was slightly stiff. "Your niece first, of course," he told her, and waited for her to lead the way as she always had. But she did not move.

"Maria Antonia told me all of it. We talked until very late last night while you slept. We have an obligation, Doctor. You probably saved more than one life by killing that man, but there can be no question that you saved the life of Maria Antonia."

He looked down. Homer's gun was hanging in front again, pulling at his trousers. He unbuckled the shell belt and tossed the equipment on the red cushions. He felt five pounds lighter.

"*D'nada*," he told her. "You owe me nothing. There is no obligation."

"There must be," she said almost tersely. "That man was *muy matador*. Everyone knows it. You did a service and we owe you for that."

George massaged the back of his neck with one hand and eyed Doña Teresa Maria. She was right about one thing, the man had indeed been a killer. He continued to eye the almost ascetic features while wondering if anyone had ever won an argument with Doña Teresa Maria. Probably not, so he changed the subject, lapsing into English.

"No obligation, ma'am, but you could grant me a favor."

She nodded almost imperceptibly, still standing regally erect and expressionless. "Name it, Doctor."

He stopped rubbing his neck, letting the hand fall to his side, and said, "Smile."

Teresa Maria's eyes widened. She stared at George for several seconds, then smiled. He smiled back at her. "You ought to do that more often, ma'am. You are a beautiful woman when you smile."

He left her standing there and went down the domed hallway to her niece's room. The door was open. He walked in and met the dark gaze of the beautiful woman in the bed. He smiled at her and she smiled back. She said, "George, you don't look like the same man. You shaved and washed and your mouth is better. There is almost no swelling."

He went to the side of the bed. "How do you feel?"

"Fine. I think I slept nearly as long as you did."

He leaned down. "Breathe, please."

She obeyed, and as he was straightening up she said, "We are back where we were?"

He went to lean on the back of a chair. "I don't know. We probably never will

215

be. I know I won't be."

She paused before speaking again. "Do you remember what you told me last night when you thought Stoll would kill us both?"

He remembered very well. "Yes."

". . . Would you say it again?"

Now he felt color coming into his face. "I said I thought you were the most beautiful woman I had ever seen."

He looked down, but she made him look up again. "Do you remember what I said? Should I say it again?"

He replied slowly. "If you wish, but last night if there had been time I would have said even more than in daylight this morning . . ."

"You wouldn't say to me?"

"I wouldn't have the nerve to say to you."

She got a twinkle in her dark eyes. "Tell me anyway."

He gripped the back of the chair, looking toward the rainstreaked window, and sounded so calm when he spoke he could have believed someone else was speaking. "I have thought about you since the first time I saw you, two years ago. I never thought of another woman like that." He tightened his grip on the chair. "I have been hopelessly in love with you that long—two years."

Silence filled the room, except for the muted

roar of the downpour. He shot her a glance, expelling his breath quietly. He recalled very distinctly what he had said to Homer at the kitchen table when Homer had hinted that George's interest in his patient was not as great as his interest in his patient as a beautiful woman. He also remembered his reply to the effect that he had nothing to offer.

He cleared his throat. "I think I'd better go over to the jacal and see how Walt is coming along."

"George, are you afraid of me?"

He had no difficulty answering this time. "No, but I was afraid to think beyond my admiration of you. Maria, I patch people up. Some days I make as much as four dollars — half of which goes to Homer." He released the back of the chair and shifted his stance slightly. "I shouldn't have told you how I feel last night, except that I didn't think it would matter and I wanted you to know before Stoll shot us. And do you know what I've done? Made a fool of myself. I can stand that; it isn't the first time and probably won't be the last time — but I've created a situation between us that can destroy a friendship."

There was a slight rustling sound in the doorway. George turned his head. Doña Teresa Maria was standing there. He had no idea how long she had been there or how much she had heard.

He walked quickly out of the room.

He had no hat, so he took a sombrero he had noticed hanging on a rack near the front door. He also buttoned his coat to the neck before opening the door. The patio was under three inches of water; another two inches and it would seep beneath the front door into the house. The downpour was continuing, but by the time he reached the patio gate he thought he could detect a lessening of the storm's force.

He made it to the barn. Juan Esteven was leaning inside, gazing over the drowned countryside. Old David Lord, who had lived through many of these torrential South Desert downpours, had built his barn on higher ground. Not much higher, but high enough; the lake in the yard lacked six or seven inches of flooding the interior. When George walked in and shook like a dog, Juan Esteven grinned – not at the wetness but at the huge hat he was wearing. Over the sound of rain atop the barn he said, "Vaquero!" and laughed.

They went together to the house where Walt had spent the night on his pallet. Inside, Walt was the only occupant. The owner of the house had gone elsewhere, to stay with a worried daughter whose jacal had a lower floor.

Walt was sitting at the only table in the house. When his visitors came stamping in he raised a hand in greeting. George looked for candles, lit two, and took them to the table. Barnard's bandage had been changed. There was no blood showing through. In fact, although his face was discolored and swollen beneath the bandage, he could speak. As George was making an examination Walt said, "She's a tough old soul an' more than likely a witch, but for a fact half the swelling's gone. She said tomorrow she'd close the holes and get the full healin' under way." He waited until George had moved around in front of the table where they could see each other, then he said, "She knows more about healin' than folks know back in Missouri."

George accepted that and went to stand in front of the corner hearth, where coals glowed. He had not been worried about Walt, and right now he was having trouble concentrating on his injury. He could still see Doña Teresa Maria standing in that doorway, as bleak-looking as an avenging angel.

Juan Esteven knew where there was a jug of red wine and brought it to the table. He and Walt sipped. Walt could not chew solid food but he had little difficulty taking liquids.

George listened to the mayordomo's description of the funeral and how wet everyone had got on the ride back. He heard Juan mention Carter Alvarado and his attention returned to the little room.

"They lost Kandelin, that's all I know. Don Alvarado was having his men spread wide and sweep the land. He was very angry and did not want to talk, but he told me they had the other two."

George went to the table and sat down. "Who are they?" he asked.

Esteven answered calmly. "One of them was the man who owns the general store in town. The other one was a disagreeable old man with dark sleeve protectors who works as a clerk in the store. Don Alvarado caught them in town, at the general store. Marshal Kandelin was with them. The marshal saw them coming from the front window and ran out the back. They had not found him when I met Don Alvarado as we were leaving town for the ranch. Maybe they will never find him, who knows?"

George frowned at the mayordomo. "That old man who works at the emporium? That's hard to believe."

Juan shrugged. "It's always hard to believe old men do bad things. It seems that when someone has one foot in the grave and the other on a banana peel, it would be better to use one's time making his peace and doing penances. Well, gringos are different, aren't they?"

George did not agree with that, but he let it pass. He knew the proprietor of the general store, Sam Goldsmith, only very casually. He did not live in Lordsville, he lived up north in one of the large cities. The vinegary clerk ran the place for Goldsmith—had run it for him for many years, if local gossip was to be believed.

"Goldsmith was in town, Juan?"

Esteven looked ruefully at George. "He must have been, if Don Alvarado and his riders caught him there. That's all I know, amigo. . . . Listen. The rain is letting up."

It was true, it was not only slackening, it was doing so much faster than usually happened. They knew why when a furious gust of wind rattled the door, making the candles gutter, and sped by.

Walt sipped wine with great care, watching the candles. "We can find him, George," he finally said. "I don't give a damn where he goes, we can find him."

Juan Esteven cocked a skeptical eyebrow. "Unless the storm caught him, how will you get him if he went down over the line into Mexico?"

Walt Barnard's blue eyes did not waver from the mayordomo's face. "We can go down over the line too."

Estevan reached for the wine jug and said no more.

CHAPTER 18

A TIME OF
DISCOMFORT

Juan Esteven thought it had been brave talk as he returned to the yard and studied the sky with its rising and empty clouds being shredded by that high wind. This was a huge territory; if Marshal Kandelin had eluded Don Alvarado and his vaqueros yesterday, how could Walt and Dr. Brunner find a man whose tracks would be under water and who had a twenty-four-hour start, even if they rode out this very instant?

Juan Esteven returned to the barn, where other vaqueros were huddling like sheep. He would find chores for them — he would not have them ride out, because even though the runoff was permitting bare patches of ground to show, he was a cautious man.

The wind was fitful, fierce and cold. It also

had strength enough to make anyone walking through it have to bend forward.

It worried at loose boards, whipped stove smoke away almost before it cleared chimneys and stovepipes. The wind and the rain also accomplished something else; the air was swept clean. Visibility was so perfect that distances seemed to be telescoped. That knoll where the duplication of sounds from the yard had been reproduced with such fidelity seemed a hundred yards closer than it was. A hundred miles of open country that had been swathed in dancing heatshimmer only a day or two earlier, so that the farther one looked the more vague and unreal the world had seemed, was now clearly discernible even in very small detail.

An old man, tall and very dark with startlingly white hair, came to the house where Walt and George Brunner were and put several manzanita faggots he'd brought into the fireplace. He smiled a little uncertainly and would have departed, but George stopped him with a question.

"*Viejo,*" he said in Spanish. "My companion here had a horse."

The old man nodded. "Yes. It is in the barn in a stall. But for riding, mister, this is terrible weather, and your companion has an injury."

Walt spoke despite his bandaged face but

since he spoke English and the old man showed by his embarrassed smile that he did not understand, George repeated what Walt had said in Spanish. "The wound is a long way from his heart, and an even greater distance from his behind, which he uses on a saddle."

The old man nodded about that, too. "Yes," he paused in uncertainty, shrugging eloquently. "It is not for me to say, señores, except that the curandera will become angry."

After the old man departed Walt got to his feet to hunt up his coat, gun belt, and weapon.

On their way through mud to the barn a vaquero Juan Esteven had put to oiling harness saw them coming. He dried both hands on his trouser legs and watched; then he went quickly to find the mayordomo.

George's sorrel was ready to be led out for saddling. So was Walt's horse with the spidery brand. They had spent a long, black night in restless anticipation of disaster, especially after the thunder had terrified them. They were willing to leave this place.

Both men mounted inside the barn, crossing the yard on horseback to the big house. There, Walt held George's reins while the doctor went to the house. The old gun and shell belt were still where he had tossed them. As he was buckling the belt beneath his coat, Teresa Maria appeared in the entrance to the room. She walked closer, and when she spoke George turned. He had not heard her coming.

"You are leaving?" she asked in English.

"Yes. Walt Barnard and I."

"In this weather, Doctor?"

He smiled wryly at her. "Yes, in this weather. Will you tell your niece I will return as soon as I can?"

"You could tell her, Doctor."

They exchanged a long look before George said, "Señora . . ."

She smiled. "I understand. I will tell her."

For the first time he warmed to her as a person. It occurred to him that whatever else inherently ruled her existence, she retained a tenderness for lovers. He wanted to say something about this to her, but he was unable to think of a way. He held out his hand. She held it briefly, and they parted.

George was unprepared for the change when he stepped out into the patio. The sun was up there, and with no filtering dust to trap its brilliance it looked five times its normal size, and the heat it hurled earthward had the ground steaming.

Walt handed back the rawhide reins and they rode from the yard southeastward, Walt setting their course. A mile out he shed his jacket, wagging his head at the humidity. "Damnedest country I was ever in," he said. "Drown a man one day and burn holes through him the next." George said there were worse territories. To that Walt made a short retort. "Yeah, where they send three bushwhackers out to kill a man, an' when he kills them it's called murder an' they got the guts to offer a five hundred dollar reward for him."

George let that pass. He did not want to hear about those three killings up in Nebraska. "Southward? You think he aimed for the border?"

"George, what would you do? In Mexico I doubt that they care one way or another what a fugitive has done, as long as he spends money down there and stays out of trouble. In any other direction Kandelin would have to worry — no matter how far he went — that there'd be a wanted dodger put out on him before long." Walt turned his bandaged face to eye George thoughtfully. "I got an idea they'd welcome someone like you down there with open arms. Those old women who plaster mud and chicken guts on wounds couldn't hold a candle to someone who has been trained as a real doctor."

Behind Walt's words had been a trace of Walt's earlier suspicion. George wagged his head. "I told you, I'm not a fugitive from anything — the law or anything else."

Walt changed the subject. "All right. About Kandelin, how far do you reckon he could get before the storm hit?"

George had no idea. He'd had no previous experience with fugitives, although lately it seemed fate had decided he needed some education in this area. Thinking back to the fury of the storm when it was at its worst, he doubted that a mounted man could have gone very far, even if he thought he was being pursued and despite a feeling of desperation.

He made a guess anyway. "To the nearest shelter."

Walt looked at him again, impassively but with interest. "For someone who's never had to run you think like someone who has. He went to shelter sure as hell. If I didn't figure that, I'd say we might as well head for town and get by a stove. The next thing, then, is where is shelter south from Lordsville?"

George did not know that either. "I've never been more than ten miles south of Lordsville." He squinted at Walt. "A ranch? Maybe some old abandoned jacal?"

Walt nodded. "Yeah. So that's what we got to watch for. Only he won't still be there." Walt cocked his eye at George again. He seemed upon the verge of making a dry comment, but then he sighed and straightened forward in the saddle. "If he didn't go on south until this morning, I'd say he left tracks," he said. "Deep, good ones, in fact. The trick'll be to find 'em, and to be sure they belong to Kandelin."

They rode steadily for two hours, studying a countryside below Lordsville neither of them had seen before. They had the north-south stage road in sight on their left, but distant.

The humidity was bad, sweat dripped from their horses even at a walk, and the sun had a wilting effect. They persevered because they were stubborn men, and when George saw what appeared to be an abandoned set of warped, bone gray wooden structures perhaps a mile to their left on the far side of the stage road, they angled in that direction, drawn as much by shade as their purpose in being out there.

There was a crude hand lettered sign in Spanish nailed to a large old raffish tree at the entrance to the yard. It said simply that this was private property and belonged to Carter Alvarado. George considered the sign longer than his companion did. It seemed to signify that Alvarado was still acquiring land.

The building consisted of a three-room wooden house without windows or doors, inhabited now by a wood rat, whose huge, conical residence was squarely in the middle of the parlor, a kitchen, and a small lean-to bedroom. There had been no human inhabitants of the house in many years. The barn was also of unplaned rough boards. Sunlight had dried them too rapidly; in many places they were warped away from the studs and interior braces.

There were no tracks of any kind in the yard or anywhere else, so George did not even dismount but pushed straight on through riding southward. George speculated about Kandelin having spent the night there and having ridden on before the rain stopped. Walt did not think so; his reason had little to do with the storm. "Too close to town," he said succinctly. "If he left town yesterday afternoon he'd have been farther along."

"Then why did we come over here?" George asked irritably.

The man with the bandaged face answered matter-of-factly, "Because we're not goin' to leave one single damn stone unturned."

For the first time George wondered why Walt, who did not know Maria Antonia and who barely knew George, was willing to risk his life to go after the man responsible for her shooting. But he dismissed the question from his mind.

They crossed the road to the west side again and when they had gone four miles they saw a dilapidated, forlorn little adobe cube some distance to their right, up ahead another mile or two.

Walt was more interested this time. As they were approaching the deserted building some magpies sprang into flight from the top of a cottonwood tree. They scolded the approaching horsemen as they fled.

George was about to dismount to explore on foot when Walt spoke. "Look inside. I think you'll find where a horse stood for a long while. There should be droppings."

George swung to the ground, eyeing his companion. Walt pointed with a gloved hand. There were horseshoe marks in the mud on the south side of the shack.

As George approached the doorless opening of the jacal his companion dismounted and walked around to the far side of the house.

Walt had been right; someone had recently taken shelter in the mud house, with his saddle animal. George returned to the yard as Walt came around the side of the jacal. He asked if someone had spent the night inside, and as George nodded Walt said, "He left good sign. Trouble is — was it Kandelin or some range-rider who got caught out here when the storm hit?"

George was beginning to get the hang of this. He said, "We're going south anyway."

Walt seemed satisfied with that answer, and as they went southward, paralleling the very distinct horseshoe prints, he said, "It sure would help if we knew how far ahead he is, because in this kind of open country, if he looks back an' we're closer than he'd like we damn well might ride right into his gunsights."

George scanned the sun-bright land. There were no places within his sight where a mounted man could hide to establish an ambush. There were only occasional bosques of trees and very little tall underbrush. Sweat made him itch and he was thirsty. There had been a dug well back at the slab-board homestead and someone had filled it with rocks, which was the best way in this kind of country to discourage squatters. If there had been a well at the jacal, he had seen no sign of it.

He worried about his horse.

The sun rose steadily, seeming to hang directly overhead for a very long time before grudgingly beginning its westerly descent.

The land was subtly changing. Even though the rain had loosened the two-inch hardpan topping to enable new growth to appear — at this time of the year mostly wildflowers of varieties one never saw anywhere but on the desert after a summer storm — as yet there was no evidence that wildflowers, or even long-dormant hummocks of buffalo grass, were germinating; the farther south they rode the more desolate and hostile the country appeared to be.

There were no habitations, although George thought there would eventually be, and he was correct. But as they plodded on the trail of someone heading straight south, what worried him even more than the heat, thirst, and desolation was the possibility that they were not on Marshal Kandelin's trail at all.

Walt was beginning to feel the sting and burn of salty sweat under his bandage. It felt more like a hundred ant stings than actual pain, but it was uncomfortable and disconcerting, and he dared not scratch his face. He wagged his head at George. "Right about now," he said, "I'd trade my carbine for a trough of cold water. My face itches to beat hell."

They startled a small band of horses as they came up the near side of a swell. The horses broke away as though they were wild, but George saw shoulder brands as he and Walt stopped to watch.

The animals ran west and were still running after they had crossed the stage road. Walt spat cotton, leaned on his saddle swells, and said,

"Tell you what, George. I think we'd do better to leave the tracks for a spell and follow those horses. They're heading for something familiar, an' I sure hope it's water."

They lost sight of the running horses because they did not push their animals in pursuit — they didn't have to. The herd left a trail in the soft earth a child could have followed.

George had gone two miles west before he fretted to himself. If they had indeed been on Kandelin's trail, what they were doing now would grant the marshal even more time to escape. As for the loose stock, if they were not heading for a place where there was water, he and Walt would be even worse off than they had been.

The land was nearly barren; there were a few clumps of grass, occasional scrub-brush thickets, no trees at all. Walt stood in his stirrups occasionally, looking ahead. "Well, there's always somebody, ain't there?" he said. "No matter how bad the land, someone always wants to settle it. Look yonder to the right."

If the sunlight had not been intense and the air clear of dust particles, details of the ranch George saw would not have been distinct. As it was, even though the distance was considerable, he recognized what was someone's residence of adobe, but much larger than a jacal, and some faggot corrals to one side of a low-roofed but rather large adobe barn. There were several outbuildings, also of mud, but what held his attention longest was the tiny figure of someone closing a wide wooden gate behind the horses they had been following.

Walt shook his head without taking his eyes off the distant ranch. "Like I said, there's always someone. Look at this range; even the snakes'll be skinny."

George was watching the man by the corral. He had stopped moving when he saw them approaching. He stood like a statue until he raised a hand to pull his hat lower. George ignored Walt's comment because he was not a stockman. Nevertheless, even to his inexperienced eye, the countryside this far south was indeed desolate-appearing.

Walt tugged loose the thong on the holster holding his six-gun. That gave George an uneasy feeling. It did not have to mean anything except that as a fugitive, Walt would want to be prepared.

The distant watcher turned finally and strode briskly in the direction of his residence. When the riders were less than a half mile out he reappeared on the shaded veranda of his house, and now he was wearing a shell belt and a gun, the holster tied to his right thigh.

George glanced at his companion. Walt was squinting intently at the figure on the porch. He said nothing, and George had no idea what his companion was thinking. But as they came down to the yard Walt spoke without taking his eyes off the waiting rancher.

"I got a feelin' he don't make his living off cattle or horses. Not in this kind of land. But he's a mite off the road to be runnin' a halfway house."

George had no time to make inquiries. The man had left his veranda and was strolling in the direction of the tie rack in front of his adobe barn. He was particularly tall and he was not a young man, but he was lean and supple, along with being very dark and wrinkled in the face from long exposure to hot suns.

CHAPTER 19

WALT'S HIDDEN TALENT

George was completely unprepared for what happened.

As they rode toward the man at the tie rack Walt relaxed in his saddle and raised a hand casually to greet the older individual, who returned the gesture, losing some of his stiff watchfulness.

They halted, and George had a moment to study the older man. He could have been forty or sixty-five. His hair was shot through with gray, and his face was leathery and lined. His physique, his slouch, even his work-scarred hands were contradictions; he had the limberness of a young man, as well as the build of one — otherwise, he looked old. When he smiled at them his teeth, though worn, were strong and even. He said, "Light, gents," and gestured.

"There's a trough around back. The water's cold."

George noticed the stranger's interest was almost exclusively in Walt. The doctor led his sorrel behind Walt and the older man down through the barn and out back, where those corralled horses were lined up like crows on a tree limb, watching everything.

The trough was old, crudely made of local rocks and mortar, with water running in at one end and leaking out at the opposite end. And it was indeed cold. As George slipped the bridle to water his horse, Walt did the same, saying, "We're right obliged to you, mister. My partner an' I been as dry as a corn husk since early morning."

The older man said, "My name is Grant Osborne."

Walt nodded. "There here is Dr. Brunner. I'm Walt Barnard. We're headin' south in a kind of a hurry, Mr. Osborne."

The older man's gaze went to George and remained there. "What kind of a doctor, friend?"

Walt spoke first. "Medical doctor. He can patch folks up when no one else can. A real, honest-to-god medical doctor, Mr. Osborne."

The older man's pale eyes lingered on George. "Is that a fact? I got to apologize, but you see I have a hell of a time rememberin' names. What was it?"

George answered shortly. "George Brunner."

Grant Osborne's interest seemed to increase by the moment. He smiled at George. "Quite a few come through, gents, and they come in all colors, sizes, and whatnot, but I never had a real, gen-u-wine doctor come through before." He continued to smile, but his eyes narrowed speculatively. "Headin' south in a sort of hurry, eh? Well now, gents, I can offer grub an' water and a place to stay where no one'll come onto you. Can even guide you on down to the line if it comes to that."

Walt studied Osborne's face and said, "I expect you'll have a fee."

Grant Osborne turned his attention back to Walt. "Well, yes, an' I'd want to know is anyone hot behind you? Boys, with the ground moist and all, if there's possemen or maybe a U.S. marshal back a ways, I'd have to know."

Walt shook his head as his horse raised its head to drip water and eye the mustangs whose faces showed above the faggots of the desert corral. "No one's behind us, Mr. Osborne. We been three weeks on the move, sashaying to lay down a false trail. I expect there was someone back there for a while, but we haven't see hide nor hair of them for more'n ten days. That'd make a difference in the fee, would it?"

Osborne smiled. "More'n just the fee, Mr. Barnard. I wouldn't want the risk if there was maybe a posse trackin' you right into my yard."

Walt was understanding. "Mr. Osborne, along with not wantin' to get you into trouble with the law, we wouldn't have in mind lyin' over for a day or two to rest the horses if we had anyone close behind us. About that fee."

Osborne squinted in the direction from which Walt and George had come. "We can talk inside the barn," he said, and led the way. It was fifteen degrees cooler inside. The older man pointed out empty stalls and stood by watching as the horses were offsaddled and turned in. He eyed Walt narrowly. "That horse you're riding, friend, has the mark of a rich cowman up north above Lordsville. If you stole him —"

"Bought him," Walt lied. "Paid in gold coin for him from a Mexican with a fancy saddle and bridle. Horse bucked him off. Didn't hurt him, but sure made him mad. He seemed to me to have a real temper. I helped him up, George here looked him over for busted bones, then we offered to hold the horse while he got back up there. But he wouldn't do it. I traded him my gentle bay horse an' gave him thirty dollars to boot. Mr. Osborne, we don't steal horses."

The older man grinned at Walt. "That's a good way to be, gents. Mind tellin' me what you do for a living?"

Walt did not even hesitate or blink. "We rob banks, sometimes stages. But banks pay a lot better."

Osborne continued to grin, but now his little pale eyes brightened with what George was sure had to be cupidity. He said, "I'll fork some feed to the horses, then we can go set on the porch and talk."

Walt stopped Osborne. "You haven't mentioned your fee. We'd like to know."

Osborne continued to grin, eyes shrewdly narrowed. "Well now, don't you boys worry about that."

Walt persevered. "We're not worrying about it, but we'd like to know what hiding us out is going to cost."

Osborne flicked a look at George, then back to Walt.

"What happened to your face?"

"Got shot through it. In one cheek and out the other one. About that fee . . ."

The old man stood in silence for a moment. "First, you got to understand there is a hell of a risk to me while you're here," he said. "Then there's the chance that if they ever catch you, you might tell about me lookin' out for

241

you. You see this land? I can't run cattle down here and the horses don't hardly pay me to keep them. Fifteen dollars a day for each one of you. Now, before you get mad, let me tell you that I put up a feller for less than one day. He left about two, three hours ago. He was in a hurry to get down over the line into Mexico, an' he give me a hundred dollars. For less than one day. So you can see I'm offerin' you boys a rock-bottom price. Thirty dollars a day for the pair of you, and we'll leave the horses in the barn where no one'll see them. And I'll feed you real good in the deal."

Both Walt and George were staring at Grant Osborne. He continued to grin at them; then the grin was gone. "You got the money, gents?" he asked.

Walt tapped his middle. "Yes. In a money belt under my clothes." He looked at George. "Partner, what do you think?"

George, who had been completely unprepared for any of this and who had grudgingly admired the way Walt had handled it, simply bobbed his head up and down.

Grant Osborne smiled. He had been running a fugitive shelter for more than a year. He'd seen the advantages about the time his income from ranching diminished to the starvation point. Over the past eight or ten months he'd

242

cursed himself many times for not having realized how the strategic location of his starve-out ranch could make him well off. "One day payment in advance," he told them.

Walt shrugged and plunged a hand into a trouser pocket. "For that kind of money I don't have to pull out the belt," he said, sounding almost disdainful. He counted out thirty greenbacks and pressed them into the outstretched hand of Grant Osborne.

As the older man stuffed the money away, he said, "Let's go get somethin' to eat, gents. Then I'll ride out to scout around an' make sure there's no one sneaking around. When I get back, maybe if you boys are of a mind, we can have a little poker session."

Walt was agreeable, but he said that first he and the doctor would go back to the trough where his partner could examine the wound and change the bandages. "Go ahead and rustle up the grub," he said to Osborne. The older man nodded briskly and left the barn in the direction of the house.

Walt did not look at George, but jerked his head for George to follow. Neither of them said a word until Walt was peeling off the bandage beside the trough. The mustangs lined up again to watch.

Walt leaned down so George could look at

the healing wounds. He said, "I believe you, George. You aren't down here because the law's after you. No one could have looked like you did in the barn if they'd ever had to lie their way out of bad trouble." He squinted one eye at George's face. "You want to guess who that man was Osborne got the hundred dollars from?"

George said, "Hold still. Bend lower. I'm going to sluice water over your face. Lower. Good. Now hold still."

Walt, bending far over, asked how the wounds looked.

George's answer was slow in coming and it wasn't really an answer. "What did she put on you?"

"She didn't tell me an' I never asked, but it smelled of sheep fat. Why, is it bad?"

"No. Your wounds are already healing, and you only got shot yesterday."

"Is that unusual?"

"Look at your arm where the nail ripped you. That happened three weeks ago, and it won't be as healed as these wounds are."

Walt said no more, because unless he held his mouth closed the rinse water ran into it. George did not want to use the same bandages, so he left Walt dripping over the trough and went searching through the barn. He found some clean wool wraps, of the kind horsemen might use for bowed tendons. He also found a clean piece of faded gingham and held it up. It was – or had been once – a woman's skirt. He left the wool inside and returned to the trough with the skirt. He held it down where Walt could see it. "I never saw a gingham bandage before, did you?" George asked.

Walt stared, then made a short reply. "Just put the damn thing on." As George was working, he said, "If we'd stayed on those tracks, sure as hell they would have made a big sashay somewhere and led us straight to this place."

"You don't know it was Kandelin," stated George, tightening the cloth.

Walt agreed. "No, I don't. I don't know it was the tooth fairy neither, but Osborne is going to tell us. Two hours head start is not so bad. We'll eat, act tired to get him to show us to some bunks, then when he makes his scout up our back trail, we'll cut loose from here. All right?"

George finished with the fresh bandage, more intrigued by the condition of Walt's wound than he was with what Barnard had just said. He stepped back to study his handiwork. "I wish I knew what the curandera put into that salve, Walt."

Walt straightened up, moving his jaw gently

to test for pain. There was almost no pain at all. He raised a hand to examine his bandage and regard what was left of the gingham skirt. This time the bandage was tighter, which hindered his speech, but he spoke anyway, sounding as though he were mumbling.

"Ask her some day. Now, you leave the talkin' to me."

George washed his hands at the trough. "Glad to," he retorted. "You're a source of constant amazement to me. You lie so well maybe I'll never be sure when you're telling the truth."

Walt straightened to his full height and looked coldly at the shorter man. "Doctor, let me tell you a simple fact of life. Lyin' has its uses, like now, or when your life is at stake. An old man told me once that if the good Lord hadn't wanted folks to lie, he'd never have taught them how."

George dried both hands on a blue bandana, returning it to his pocket and smiling at Walt. "You're dead right." He pocketed the handkerchief and shoved Homer's gun and holster from in front back to where it belonged on his right side. Walt watched this, and as they were walking back up through the barn he veered off, cut a tie-string off an old Texas A-fork saddle, sank to one knee, and using the hole in the bottom of Homer's holster to insert one end of the thong through, lashed the gun in place by securing it to Dr. Brunner's leg. As he stood up he said, "Don't they teach you fellers anything except how to sew people up in medical school?" Before George could reply, Walt led the way into the humid, very hot yard.

Over at the main house, Grant Osborne appeared on the shaded porch. "Come along, gents," he called to them. "It's ready. Antelope steaks fried with onions, fried spuds like my late wife taught me to make, bless her soul, an' a fresh pot of coffee with a little pulque to give it muscle."

Osborne was smiling right up until Walt and George mounted the steps to his porch; then he said, "Where did you get that cloth for his bandage, Doctor?"

"In your medicine box in the barn. We'll pay you for it."

Osborne did not say another word as he led them inside his blessedly cool large old adobe residence, which smelled wonderfully of food and hot coffee.

CHAPTER 20

INTO A HOSTILE LAND

Something occurred to George Brunner he had wondered about several times in his life: Osborne, who looked like any other hard-rock rancher, and whose principles had probably been the first casualty in his hard life, was a phenomenally fine cook, even though his antelope steaks did not resemble any steaks George had ever eaten.

Osborne beamed when George complimented him on his cooking. Whatever else the lean, rough-looking older man was or had been, what he probably should have been was a professional chef. His was a talent extremely few people possessed. Instead of operating a halfway ranch — halfway between U.S. law and the border — Osborne should have gone east, where his talent would have provided him with a better living, more comfort, and certainly less risk.

They ate and talked, and when they got down to coffee, George got another surprise; his coffee was not bitter, and it had the faintest hint of mint to its taste. He had never tasted such coffee before. Even Walt, whose palate had been damaged long ago, savored the coffee, although he said nothing about it. He was busy working the conversation around in a very circuitous way to the identity of that man who had left a couple of hours earlier.

Osborne laced his coffee with pulque, which his guests declined. He evidently was a drinking man. He sat back, alternately sipping his coffee and sucking his teeth, eyes bright and cheeks slightly flushed beneath their leathery tan. "I got a rule," he explained to Walt. "If someone drifts in tomorrow or next week askin' if maybe I had a couple of strangers, one of them a medical doctor, visitin' the ranch I say no, I never had no such visitors." Osborne smiled and drank more laced coffee. "You'll understand that, Mr. Barnard."

Walt had to admit that he did indeed understand it, but he then asked a question that indicated that understanding Osborne's tact had not moved him away from what was on his mind. He said, "Just curious is all. When we were sidling around that town up yonder, Lordsville, there was some kind of ruckus going on. Some Mex cowboys and that feller I traded out of the horse was raisin' hell and proppin' it up. We didn't go in and ask what the trouble was. We was trying to get on past. Just as soon not have to answer questions. But those cowboys was fanning out all over the place and we met one of them. He said the town marshal had turned out to be mixed up in some kind of attempt to steal a big ranch, and they'd scairt him off and were looking for him. Would it have been the marshal, eh, Mr. Osborne?"

The older man drained his coffee cup and smiled broadly. "Y'know how it is in this life, Mr. Barnard. A man works from dawn until dark just to scrape out a living."

George had already decided that Grant Osborne liked his pulque, and that he'd taken on a fair load of it in the coffee, so he attributed his last remark to that. But Walt Barnard, who was sitting slouched across the table from the older man, interpreted Osborne's statement differently and tossed a ten-dollar greenback in front of Osborne.

The older man eyed the money, his smile fading, and eyed Walt too. "One question," he said softly. "You told me the truth down in the barn — you boys raided a bank somewhere an' want to get down over the line? You're not lawmen?"

Walt snorted. "Lawmen? Mr. Osborne I been called a lot of bad names, but no one ever called me that before. Hell no, we're not lawmen."

Osborne's hand closed around the greenback. It was whisked off the table as the older man's eyes puckered nearly closed with his crafty smile. "Yes, sir. That's who he was. Name is Kandelin. He was town marshal up yonder for a long time. I never liked the man, to tell you the gospel truth. We never had any run-ins, but that's because I don't go near Lordsville if I can keep from it. But I know of things he's done to other folks." The crafty smile deepened. "But you know how it is; a man can overlook a lot of dislike for a hundred dollars."

Walt nodded his head as though in agreement, and refilled his coffee cup. Osborne offered to lace the java. Walt shook his head. "Never drink before sundown," he said, and looked around the cool, gloomy room. "I ate too much. You got bunks where a man could rest for a couple of hours?"

Osborne took them to the back of the house, where there was one very large room with several iron cots in it. There was also one chair.

Otherwise the room was bare. There was one of those grilled windows in the south wall and someone had hung an old blanket beside it which could be pulled in front of the window to block out daylight. Osborne gestured. "Settle in, gents. I got to feed your horses and make my scout. I'll be back in an hour or so. Sooner, if I see a posse." He smiled, this time with no mirth. "I sure hope you boys was tellin' the truth about not havin' anybody up your back trail."

Walt tossed his hat aside and went to sit on the edge of an iron cot. "We told you the truth," he said.

Osborne nodded his head, little eyes speculative. "Good. When I get back maybe we can have a game or two of poker."

Walt nodded and Osborne left the room on his way back through the house to the shaded veranda. Walt went over to close the door. He eyed George ruefully. "You're right. He's one hell of a cook. I got a notion that maybe Judas might have been, too." He returned to the cot and sat down. "Don't get comfortable. We'll give him a while to get out a ways, then we'll see if we can make up the time Kandelin's got in a lead on us."

George watched Walt roll and light a smoke. He inhaled blue smoke and exhaled gray smoke. Two or three hours head start would be very difficult to overcome, and he said so. Walt agreed, mouth trickling smoke, and settled back on the cot, gazing at the ceiling. George told him he thought smoking would not be good for his wounds, and Walt replied without raising up to look at him. "Relax," he said. "There isn't a damn thing a man does that don't harm him some way."

George said no more. He, too, settled back, and as a result of the big meal, the coolness inside the house, and the silence, he would have slept if Walt had not spoken to him every five or ten minutes to keep him awake.

When the cigarette was burned down, Walt stamped on it and reached for his hat. He left the room without a word to George. After a short time he returned. "Time to go." He jerked his head at the door.

George sat up. "Suppose he's waiting in the barn to see what we'll do?"

"He's not. I saw him a long way off riding in a big half circle from west to east. All we got to do is kept the barn between us and him."

They went down to the barn and entered from out back. The mustangs lined up to stand and watch as they had done before. Saddling did not take long. Both the sorrel and Walt's horse had been fed, watered, and rested. They were ready as they were led out back to be mounted.

Walt made a final tour up toward the front of the barn, looking for Osborne. When he returned he nodded to George and mounted. They not only kept the barn between them and anyone who might be watching from far out, they also keep the house behind them.

The heat was waiting, and it had not diminished, even though the sun was slanting away. By the time Walt found what he thought would be Marshal Kandelin's tracks, George had sweat running under his shirt again.

The land a few miles south of the Osborne ranch began to show vestiges of genuine desert; scaly rocks, stunted underbrush, patches of barren ground of considerable extent, and tiny wildflowers that had popped up where their seeds had been dormant for a year. They would proliferate over the next week or so, and when the last moisture was sucked out of the soil, they would die for another year. George had time to reflect on this natural phenomenon; Walt was studying the onward flow of country and the tracks they were following. If he noticed the flowers he gave no indication of it, and he had very little to say until shadows were puddling on the lee side of stone ledges and thickets of scrub underbrush.

Walt led the way down into a rough, rock-strewn arroyo, dismounted, loosened his cinch, and leaned on the saddle, eyeing his companion. "Seems to me there's only two kinds of men. Those that are hunted and those that do the hunting. I never been on this end before."

For the second time George wondered why Walt was doing this, but he said nothing.

"Rough country, George. Hard on horses. I had a notion it'd be more sandy and flat. Wherever the marshal is, if he sees us, he won't have any trouble settin' up an ambush." Walt paused to range a look from narrowed eyes to the left and right, and dead ahead. "It would help like hell if just one of us had been down here before, because I got a feelin' Kandelin has, and that's an advantage. But . . ." He looked over as George also swung down and loosened his own cinch. "But I got an idea. We got his tracks to follow, and he'll know that. I think we'd do better to just slouch along. Don't make him think we're really pushing it."

George found a flaw in that. "And he'll get even farther ahead. I don't think the border is far from here, Walt. Maybe by morning he'll cross it."

Walt nodded. "Yeah, he might. But we're goin' to rest the horses often, an' when he stops to rest after nightfall we're goin' to keep right on going. *If* he stops to rest, which he may not do if he sees us back here. But even if he doesn't, if he keeps going after dark, he'd better have a horse made of iron. This sure as hell isn't a country I'd want to be afoot in because I rode a horse until he dropped."

They left the arroyo, picked up the trail again, and continued to move, but without any haste. George reviewed what Walt had said and found about as many reasons for the idea not to work as he found reasons it might work. But he kept this to himself. Walt was more knowledgeable in this matter, but most important to their success, Walt had not theorized as much as he had put experience to work. A fugitive learned many lessons as he went along, or he got caught. Walt had covered a lot of country from Nebraska to the South Desert without being caught.

George's lack of confidence equalled his fatigue. That was another thing that intrigued him about his companion. Even though Walt looked ludicrous with a bandage of gingham skirting on his face and had not rested for any length of time since they'd ridden from the Lord ranch yard, to Georges trained eye Walt was no more tired now than he had been very early that same morning.

The rough countryside got rougher. They

encountered tarantulas as large as a man's fist and ten times as hairy. They also saw Gila monsters — large, sluggish-acting, lizardlike venomous creatures whose tiny legs were out of proportion to the thickness of their orange-mottled bodies.

And, they saw small foxes — very few, however, and never as more than a blur of movement through the underbrush. At one halt to rest the horses, they ran afoul of a greenish-hided rattlesnake, not very long but as thick as a man's wrist. The snake was snugged back in camouflaging shade at the base of a thornpin bush, its lidless eyes watching their every move. They would not have noticed the snake except that one of the horses ducked its head and blew its nose. The snake raised its spiky tail and rattled a warning. Walt, in the act of rolling a smoke, froze, waited a moment, then very slowly moved only his head. George's reaction was similar. Even though he had never had a close encounter with a rattlesnake, instinct told him what to do, and moving fast was not part of it.

Walt located the serpent, studied it, and went back to rolling his cigarette. "I stepped on one of them once," he said dryly.

"What happened?"

"Nothing. It threshed around and tried to

bite the toe of my boot. I kept standing on him until he was dead." Walt lit up and considered the snake. "He looks like a timber rattler. They got that green look to them, and they're usually big around and short. But what in hell would a timber rattler be doing in this country?"

George had no idea. As the rattler slithered away, the doctor turned his attention to the increasingly inhospitable land southward. There were upright plinths, in some instances as tall as a mounted man. And there was cactus. Except for one or two varieties, it seemed to grow in communal clumps.

In every part of the country he had been in, there had been distinctive varieties of vegetation; fir trees at high elevations, pine trees lower down, distinctive kinds of berry bushes, flowers that only throve in special areas. The desert was no exception; it had some especially localized forms of underbrush, cactus, and its own unique scenery and views. It occurred to him that the farther south they went, the more greenery they encountered, until, as now, it was difficult to see ahead more than a hundred or so yards unless there was a bare place.

Where, he asked himself, would Kandelin be?

"After we get this son-of-a-bitch, then what?" Walt asked, stamping out his cigarette.

George turned. "After we get him? You mean *if* we get him."

Walt's narrowed, hat-brim-shaded eyes ranged ahead as he replied to that. "We'll find him. I told you at the Lord place we can get him. Maybe we'll have thick tongues and be sweated down ten pounds, but we'll get him." He glanced in George's direction again. "Then what? I mean, after we tote him back to Lordsville, then what?"

George reflected calmly that out here in the middle of nowhere with no assurance they would both ride back if they found the town marshal, it seemed very premature to think about the future, so he said, "We'll have to wait and see."

Walt looked away. "I don't much care for this country down here, but back up around Lordsville, it's good country. I'd like to settle up there. But that's pointless to think about, isn't it?"

"Why?"

"What d'you mean, 'why'? You're the one that told me Marshal Kandelin had a reward poster on me. I got to move on. Most likely I'll always have to move on."

One of their horses threw its head up, little ears forward. Both men tried to locate what had caught its attention and was still holding it.

Neither of them could spot anything. Walt said they had rested long enough, and besides, he didn't like the idea of standing like a damn target, so they snugged up cinches, rode back to the drying horseshoe marks, and continued on south.

George, watching the onward country, thought back to the meal Grant Osborne had cooked for them and commented on it. His companion, also watching the land ahead and riding slouched, agreed that he couldn't remember ever having eaten such a meal. Then Walt said, "Did you see some fresh-cut stud colts among his mustangs?"

George had not noticed, neither could he see what that had to do with what they were discussing, until Walt gave George an amused look and said, "That's what you ate."

George stared. "What are you talking about?"

"What do they call testicles in Spanish?"

"*Cojones*," George replied, and left his mouth open as he stared. "No," he exclaimed. "He said it was antelope steak."

"Yeah. Well, partner, if he'd told you what it really was, would you have eaten it?"

George did not reply. He simply rode along, mouth agape, staring at Walt.

Walt solemnly nodded his head. "That's what you ate, partner."

"I don't believe it. How do you know?"

"Well, for one thing, I saw the altered colts. For another thing, I've eaten them before — from bull calves mostly, but also a few times from stud colts."

George faced forward again. He remembered being curious, because antelope steaks were flat, like beefsteak. He said, "Gawd," and Walt laughed, which did not help any. George turned on him. "Why didn't you tell me?"

"I just did."

George rode in stony silence for a long time, until the shadows were firming up and the entire South Desert was beginning to acquire a mantle of even, light tan shade. But the heat did not dissipate for another two hours, until the sun was gone and a pale moon was rising.

CHAPTER 21

A RIDE TO REMEMBER

George was curious. There was a moon, which allowed limited visibility, but he wanted to see how his companion would track Kandelin after sundown.

For an hour or so Walt did it from the saddle, as he had been doing it for most of the day, except that with poorer visibility he rode hunched forward and did not talk. Later, when George could not make out the tracks about half the time, because they went through patches of loose shale or ledges of stone, his companion swung to the ground and, without losing a step, walked ahead, leading his horse. In this manner he was able to persevere. Without the moonlight, feeble though it was, he would certainly have had more difficulty.

George was tired and hungry again. Under

other circumstances he might have mentioned this, but watching Walt on foot up ahead, neither slackening his long stride nor more than very briefly taking his eyes off the shadowy trail they were following, he thought it seemed not to be the time to complain.

The early night was absolutely quiet. There was not a breath of air stirring, the sky was flawlessly clear, a million stars winked, and carrying perfectly through the pure atmosphere came the faint sound of shod hooves rattling over loose rock to their left.

Walt did not stop or look around, he simply changed course and continued on his way. They were leaving the tracks when they did this. The tracks continued directly southward. George wanted to say something, but refrained. Any sound would travel. He considered the possibilities but overlooked something: he worried it might be mustangs they'd heard, neglecting to realize a basic fact — wild horses did not wear steel shoes.

Walt walked for an hour, his odd bandage making his face appear uniquely evil by the watery moonlight. He did not say one word and he did not slacken his stride until they were on the verge of what appeared to be an extensive area of loose chat, mostly decomposed granite but with some much harder material scattered through it.

Walt paused, then turned southward. Again he hiked along effortlessly, leading his horse, but now he did not watch the ground for sign.

That worried George, so he dismounted and also walked, but George concentrated on looking for tracks. He did not find any until an hour later. With the sickle moon high, they lost the shale field, going eastward until Walt grunted and turned directly southward again. Here, finally, George felt relieved. They were again on a trail.

It bothered him that to the west, where they had been following horseshoe tracks, there had been no indication that Kandelin had turned this far eastward, but it was a shortlived cause for anxiety. Walt halted once, pointed, and resumed his walk. Tracks came eastward and cut back in the direction of the shale field. They were following the same horseman. George was relieved, even though he was still troubled by the fact that there was no actual proof they were trailing Marshal Kandelin.

However, as George had pithily said hours earlier, who in hell except Kandelin would be crazy enough to cross this stretch of desolation.

Walt did not seem to tire. George was impressed by the man's stamina. He had bullet wounds, he had probably slept badly last night if he had slept at all, and neither of them had taken any water since leaving the Osborne place, nor any food. Yet George could detect no lessening of his companion's grim perseverance, right up to the time when the moon was nearly directly above and Walt stopped so abruptly his plodding horse nearly walked up onto his heels.

Walt turned slowly and spoke in something close to a whisper. "Smell anything?"

George wrinkled his nose, then shook his head.

Walt faced forward again and squatted in front of his horse, remaining like that a long time. George tried again to detect odors. All he picked up was the very faint fragrance of tiny desert flowers.

Walt rose and stood hipshot, his left hand with the reins in it hooked in his shell belt. Without looking around at George or speaking loud enough to be heard fifteen feet away, he said, "Does Kandelin smoke?"

George tried to recall ever having seen the lawman with a stogie or a cigarette, and failed. "I don't know. Is that what you smell?"

"Yes. If it's not Kandelin, I got a halo an' wings."

George eased up beside Walt and tried again to detect an aroma. Once he thought he had,

265

but the very next moment he was certain he hadn't.

Walt thrust his reins at George. "I'm goin' ahead a piece. Don't let the horses whinny or blow their noses."

George stood with a saddle animal on each side, watching Walt turn to a fading shadow up ahead. He was moving very cautiously.

George looked at the horses. If they had detected a scent it was not one that meant much to them. They were both tired and perfectly willing to use this interlude of rest to hang their heads and catch forty winks. He thought they were also thirsty, but there was nothing he could do about that.

He looked on both sides and behind him. His feeling was of being abandoned in the middle of a totally uninhabited moonscape. By eerie starshine and moonlight the desert in every direction looked dead and endless.

He sank to one knee, and he was still resting like that when Walt returned. It could have been no one else — there probably was not another human being in a thousand miles with a bandage covering half his face made of a woman's gingham skirt.

Walt sank down and shoved back his hat, so that ghostly light highlighted the bones of his face and made the sunken places around his eyes look dark. He was tired.

"We got him," he said softly. "I think his horse gave out. It's hobbled, but it's listless when it should be lookin' for something to eat."

"Did you see him?"

Walt said, "The next time I go out of a town in this damn country an' don't carry a canteen I hope somebody strikes me dead. Yeah, I saw him — well, I saw someone rolled into a blanket sleeping in a little swale."

George nodded. "It's him," he said, surprising himself at this statement of reassurance, but he wanted Walt to be right.

Walt sat a moment considering the ground, then roused himself. "Hobbles," he muttered. There was not even a bush to tie horses to. As they were both kneeling to buckle the hobbles in place he added, "I got a hunch we're close to the border."

George said nothing.

Walt stood up, looking southward as he waited for George. He shook his head. "I'm past forty, George. That's too old for this kind of damn foolishness."

He pulled out his saddle gun and led the way southward, only once pausing to point toward the ground and gesture for silence. George continued walking, alternately watching for stones and looking ahead.

He was surprised at the distance. It had not seemed Walt could have covered so much ground in the time he had been gone. But even as he was thinking about this his partner halted, noiselessly sank to one knee, and pointed with a gloved hand.

They were slightly behind a gentle rise in the land and could see over it and down into a swale. There was a horse down there, looking directly in their direction without moving or making a sound. Several yards from the horse there was a dark lump on the leached-out gray earth.

George knelt beside Walt. The rangeman turned and smiled. The only way to be sure it was a smile was to be close enough to see the sunken eyes crinkle; the rest of Walt's face was wrapped in gingham.

George did not smile. The longer they hunkered, the more he remembered things he had heard about Frank Kandelin. George feared the man, even in his sleep. He knew from personal experience that he could beat a man senseless with his hands, and he had heard a number of stories of the marshal's ability with weapons.

Walt was leaning on his upright carbine as though it were a staff, his full attention upon the mound of bone and muscle beneath its old blanket. He did not know Kandelin personally but he knew his kind of an individual. He softly sighed and looked around once more, then raised the Winchester and held it lightly across his body, prepared to throw it instantly to his shoulder. "George, toss some stones down there." At George's questioning look, Walt said, "Do it."

There was no shortage of rocks. George picked up several, aimed, and threw a stone high. It landed fifteen feet from the lawman. The horse was momentarily diverted, but Kandelin went right on sleeping.

George pitched another stone. This one was close enough to make the horse snort and hop a few feet in the opposite direction. It probably was the snort rather than the sound of the rock falling that awakened Marshal Kandelin. He turned once, groggily pushing himself up into a sitting position. He did not seem particularly alarmed, but he had clearly been sleeping very deeply, undoubtedly as a result of the arduous day he had put in before reaching this place. That could have accounted for the way he sat there looking around without immediately reaching for the holstered Colt on the far side of his resting place.

He cleared his pipes, spat, and looked out where the horse was again standing completely still, looking in the direction of Kandelin's pursuers. By now most of the cobwebs were cleared out of his mind. He drew up a little straighter, peered in the same direction as his horse, and reached surreptitiously for the coiled shell belt and holstered Colt.

George had been engrossed in watching, so when the muzzle blast erupted beside him, he jumped. Walt levered himself up and called harshly to the floundering man in the old army blanket, whose gun and bullet belt had just been struck by a Winchester slug and hurled violently out of reach.

"Set still! You hear me? *Set still or I'll blow your head off!*"

Kandelin's astonishment was so complete that he was dumbstruck. He had been trying to kick clear of the old blanket and lunge for the distant six-gun. He was still frantic and desperate when Walt Barnard fired his second shot. This time the shell belt and holster were violently punched even farther.

Kandelin reacted to the explosion by suddenly becoming stone still, except for his head, which turned slowly in the direction of the gunman. There was a skiff of black-powder smoke hanging above Walt.

The instant there was gunfire Kandelin's ridden-down horse dug deep inside himself for the fear-inspired energy that set him hopping as fast as hobbled forelegs would allow.

He was still hopping when Walt said, "Stand up, Marshal. Keep your hands away from your sides. I said stand up!"

Kandelin obeyed. The astonishment and shock were past. As he straightened to his full, thick height, he looked beyond Walt, as though expecting to see possemen. He scowled at the second indistinct shape on the downhill side of the little swale. "Brunner? Is that you, Brunner?"

Walt answered sarcastically. "Naw, it's Billy the Kid, you miserable bastard. Now, you bend down and hoist both your trouser legs."

The lawman growled. "I don't carry no hide-out guns."

"Do it anyway," Walt retorted, and cocked his carbine.

Kandelin grunted and bent over. He drew up his left trouser leg to expose a boot top, then raised the right trouser leg. At that distance and in poor light, neither of the men just over the verge could see what the right hand was doing as the left hand pulled up the pants leg.

The explosion was accompanied by a blinding mushroom of nearly white flame. George grabbed for Homer's old six-gun as Walt squeezed off his third Winchester shot, but he, too, had been temporarily blinded. His shot missed. Before their eyes were clear, Marshal Kandelin had run up out of the shallow swale and hurled himself behind a half dead thicket of underbrush.

George got belly down. Walt did the same, swearing in a savage whisper.

George waited until the last echo had died, then yelled to Marshal Kandelin, "I can see you."

The thicket's brittle branches shook violently. Walt had three slugs left. He pumped one to the left, one to the right of Kandelin's hiding place, and drilled the third one straight down through.

The threshing increased wildly.

Walt watched for a moment, then groped around in back for the remaining six carbine cartridges he had. A roaring shout came from back in the thicket.

"Doctor! Dr. Brunner, I'm bleedin' bad."

George started to roll up to his feet, but Walt grabbed him with one hand and forced him back down. He was watching the distant thicket and did not even look at George. "Throw out your gun, Kandelin. As far as I'm concerned you can bleed to death. *Throw it out!*"

Something small and dark sailed over into the clear ground on the east side of the thicket. Walt looked at it and shook his head. "Belly gun," he muttered, and released his grip on George. "All right. We both stand up at the same time and we both go over there — like we did at the ranch — you from up here, me from farther to the left." He looked at George. "A double-barreled belly gun, the damn idiot." As Walt rose holding the carbine to plug several fresh loads past the slide his disgust rang in each word he said. "What kind of an idiot goes up against two six-guns and a Winchester with a damn two-shot hideout gun?"

George made no comment. His most vivid recollection of the terrifying interlude at the Lord ranch was of Maria Antonia lying in bed, poised with one of those little weapons as Henry Stoll dared her to try and shoot him.

They could hear Marshal Kandelin groaning in genuine pain and split wide of each other as they started for the thicket, each carrying a cocked gun.

CHAPTER 22

HEADING BACK

When George came around behind the thicket he stopped dead. There was blood everywhere. Walt's third bullet had struck the lawman high in the right leg. George went a little closer and watched the bleeding a moment. He sank down to put force on a pressure point near Kandelin's groin; the bleeding began to lessen. Kandelin was panting, his face was chalky, and he squirmed, until George looked around and said, "Give me your britches belt."

Walt complied, still ignoring the stare he was getting from the man he had shot. George looped the belt and asked Walt to find a strong, short stick. This took longer, and meanwhile George kept the pressure on as he looked into the lawman's ashen face. Kandelin's pupils were dilated, he was in a state of shock. When

Walt returned they twisted the belt and choked off the bleeding, using the stick as their fulcrum. While Walt held the stick George cut away the soggy trouser leg, used his bandana to mop the blood away, and examined the injury. He had already reached one conclusion: Walt's bullet had probably severed an artery, and if that were so, there was no way Kandelin could be taken back to Lordsville on horseback.

George was not a surgeon. Homer was, but Homer was up in Lordsville.

"You got it stopped?" Kandelin sounded hoarse.

George nodded without looking up or speaking.

"What's it look like?" the lawman asked.

This time George raised his head to meet the shock-darkened small gray eyes of the burly town marshal. "It looks like you'll be in bed for several months, if we can get you out of here and back to town. You've lost a lot of blood."

Kandelin's head sank back. He rolled it tiredly to look at Walt Barnard. "What's wrong with your face?"

"Got shot through it from one side to the other side by that killer you sent out to finish what he started at the Lord place. Your killer is dead, Marshal."

Kandelin did not seem to care, or perhaps it

went much deeper; he rolled his head in the opposite direction and let his eyes close.

George said, "We got to ease up on the tourniquet now and then, and if we do the blood's going to spurt like a busted water pipe."

Walt nodded. "Cut an artery?"

"I think so."

"Can you patch it?"

George had been speculating about this. "I could try, but it'll be a bloody mess and I don't have anything to work with. And there isn't time enough for improvising. Look at him — I don't think he'd survive. In fact, I wouldn't give much for his chances anyway."

Without using his dwindling strength to turn his head and look at them, Marshal Kandelin said, "Brunner? Never mind. I'm gettin' awful sleepy. . . . Listen to me. . . . It was Sam Goldsmith's notion. You know Sam; he owns the general store. . . . Him and that scrawny old man who clerks at the store . . . Henry Stoll an' me, but it was Goldsmith's idea . . . With her dead, Goldsmith'd put up the money to bid in Lord's Land, and when he had legal title . . . he'd carve it up. . . . My share would have been five thousand acres of land, eight hundred head of cattle . . . and fifteen thousand dollars. . . . Brunner?"

"Yes, Marshal."

"Who got Henry Stoll?"

"I did."

That brought a weak spasm of movement to the dying man. "You . . . ? In a gunfight?"

"Not exactly, Marshal. He didn't know I was in Maria Antonia's bedroom when he came to shoot her. I was behind the door."

"You shot him . . . in the back?"

"No. I called, and when he faced me I shot him. Marshal, what was he to get from the breakup of the Lord ranch?"

"Who, Henry? All the horses. Every head of loose stock. . . . Brunner . . . and my left leg feels hot. Are you doin' anything?"

George looked down, then up again. He said nothing because Frank Kandelin's eyes were half open and fixed high overhead. His jaw was slack. George eased back on his haunches, gazing at the lawman's face. When Walt said, "He looks dead," George nodded, but he told Walt to keep his grip on the stick. They sat like that for ten minutes. Then George looked down as he told Walt to ease up slowly and gently on the stick.

No blood gushed forth.

George stood up. "That's it. He's dead." As Walt got to his feet George added, "I'll go to get the horses. You stay here and get some rest. If anyone's earned it, you sure have."

Walt fished around for his makings and while gazing at the slack, ashen face of Marshal Kandelin went to work rolling a smoke. There were a number of things he would have preferred — including a full canteen of water, something to eat, maybe ten hours of uninterrupted sleep — but all he had was the cigarette, so he smoked it and turned his back on the dead man, looking for the worn-down horse.

It was cropping what grass it could find beneath scattered patches of underbrush. Rest had helped the horse recover. Walt did not go after it. That could be done later, when the animal'd had more time to get something inside his belly. Even by puny starlight it looked as gaunt as a gutted snowbird.

He heard George returning, ground his smoke underfoot, and watched the doctor ride on up. Walt's saddle had a lariat on the right side of the forks. That was the only rope they had.

Without a word they rolled the dead man into his old brown blanket and lifted him. He was much heavier than either of them had anticipated. They had to lower him, get braced, and try a second time. That time they got him across George's saddle, but the sorrel horse craned around, whiffed blood, and started to move away. They made him stand. Walt took his horse and rode out to remove the hobbles from Kandelin's horse, leading it back by the bridle reins.

He passed the reins to George and offered to help with the saddling, but George managed that by himself and swung up. He was easily forty pounds lighter on the back of the worn out horse than Kandelin would have been.

Walt led off, leading the sorrel with its inert burden. The moon had departed without its absence being noted, but the chill in the air got through Dr. Brunner's dulled senses. He looked up. It was very late; in fact, dawn was close.

An hour later Walt twisted in the saddle to speak. "I expect they've gone through his office and found that damn dodger on me."

George thought this was probably true, but all he said was, "Let's just worry about reaching town. Whatever comes next, we can start worrying about it later. I'm so damn tired I could sleep sitting up."

Walt eyed his companion for a while, then straightened forward. "I'm glad we teamed up, George," he said.

They had to stop twice to adjust the dead man, whose considerable weight had a way of shifting, regardless of how carefully they tried to lash him so that it was evenly distributed.

The last time they were doing this Walt asked if George had picked up Kandelin's little hide-out gun. George had, it was in his coat pocket. Walt asked, "Do you want it?"

George shook his head.

"Keep it for a souvenir. Those are the sorriest excuse for a weapon I ever saw in my life."

George kept silent this time, too, as Walt again expressed scorn for belly guns.

The cold increased. Both men turned up their collars and rode hunched. They saw dawn arrive with haggard, stubbly, sunken-eyed faces. Walt was peering in the direction of the Osborne ranch. "You suppose that little weasel'd feed us again?" he said.

George thought it was not very likely. "It probably worried hell out of him when he got back and we were gone."

"Have you run into men like him very much, George?"

"No. At least if I have, I didn't know it."

"He sold Kandelin out for ten dollars. He'd do the same to his own mother — maybe for even less than ten dollars. I got a grudge against fellers like him that goes back a long way. Someday I'll tell you why."

George also looked in the direction of the Osborne place, and although there was new daylight again, he could not locate the rooftops.

He said, "Walt, I'd just as soon not hear your secrets. I think you're a good man. That's the only judgment I have to make about you. The rest of it you can take to the grave with you."

Walt rode along, slouched with weariness — otherwise he might have been able to anticipate the surprise that was coming toward them on a big, rawboned dappled-gray colt. Walt did not even see the rider until George, who was farther back, called his attention to him, and by then the distant rider had boosted his horse into a lope and was bearing down on them.

Walt squinted and gave a short, alarmed grunt. George saw Walt's horse slacken and halt. The sorrel, which was plodding along half asleep, bumped him. George watched the oncoming rider and reined up beside Walt. By then they could both see the gun in Grant Osborne's fist atop his big, strong dappled colt.

It was too late to do much.

Osborne came down to a slogging walk and halted thirty feet away. His usual unctuous smile was missing, and as though to emphasise the seriousness of the situation, he cocked the handgun. He evened his weight in the stirrups, studying the dead man on the sorrel. "Well, well, gents. You told me you wasn't lawmen," he said.

Neither Brunner nor Barnard spoke.

Osborne's deeply tanned, deeply lined face settled into expressionlessness. "Dump the guns, boys. Be careful. This here gun's got a real scary trigger pull."

George tossed Homer's gun to the ground. Walt pulled out his Winchester and let it fall, then felt for his six-gun. Osborne was watching every move. He brought his gun hand forward, aiming squarely at Walt's middle.

Walt raised his Colt slowly and tossed it away. Osborne relaxed a little. He studied his captives thoughtfully for a moment, then revealed his reason for stopping them — it had nothing to do with the dead marshal or his earlier statement about them being lawmen.

"Mr. Barnard, get down off your horse."

Walt dismounted.

"Now then, Mr. Barnard, pull out your shirt and toss that money belt over here to me. . . . You don't hear real good, do you?" Osborne brought the gun forward again, tipped down this time. Osborne's perpetually squinted eyes were deathly still. "I don't care about Kandelin. Like I said, I never liked him anyway. But I like money. In fact, when I get that money belt I figure to leave this damn country and go somewhere they got trees and water and plenty of grass. You boys never told me how much is in that money belt. I been speculatin' on that since last night, when I decided to come down here and wait for you gents. How much is in it, Mr. Barnard?"

Walt spat, looked at George, then slowly back to the man on the tall dappled-gray horse. "Suppose we just divvy it up," he said, and Grant Osborne laughed. Walt made another offer. "Well then, suppose you leave us both with enough to get new duds and a week's rest at a rooming house. We been a long time without sleep, or much else."

Osborne's amusement had died. He wigwagged the gun. "Pull it out from under your shirt and pitch it over here. If you got some idea someone's goin' to happen along and save your bacon, you never been more wrong in your life. Look around this damn country. There's us three and a dead man. That's all. Mr. Barnard, I got all the time in the world, but unless you take off the damn belt and toss it to me, you don't have no more'n another minute at the most."

Walt shifted to a hipshot stance, eyeing the gun and the weasel-like dark-skinned face above it. George, feeling that Walt had done everything possible to postpone the inevitable, spoke to Osborne in a worried voice.

"He doesn't have it. I have it."

Both men turned. Walt stared, but Grant

Osborne didn't. He smiled.

"Now, why didn't you say that to start with, Doctor? All right, now you get down off that horse and step to its head where I can watch you. Get down!"

George knew Walt was staring at him as he leaned forward and swung to the ground. He had the distance between his stirrup and the horse's shoulder to get his hand on Kandelin's little gun. It had one unfired bullet. If he missed, which he thought would be what happened, Osborne would probably kill him and Walt. Osborne had either five or six slugs in his six-gun.

Aside from having the little gun with its single bullet, George had one other advantage. When he dismounted to move to the head of his horse, he would be momentarily shielded by it. It would be between him and Grant Osborne.

As a reliable basis for a ruse, George had a couple of seconds to consider how unreliable it was. He also knew instinctively, and had known since Osborne had stopped them to talk, that even if there had been a money belt, Osborne would never have allowed them to ride away after robbing them. Either way, he and Walt would end up dead.

This ruse was all they had left.

284

George came down stiffly, right hand plunging frantically into his coat pocket as his boot touched the ground. He groped, found the weapon, closed his hand around it, and was beginning to draw it as he removed his left foot from the stirrup and started toward his horse's head. He had the little gun in his fist and timed the cocking of it to the moment he appeared in full sight in front of the horse.

He saw Osborne's face, sly, dark features in their fixed-looking vacant smile, and the cocked gun aimed in his direction. He did not aim at Osborne. He did not tilt the little gun at all when he squeezed the trigger.

The muzzle blast was louder than a six-gun report would have been. The little gun bucked in George's hand as he was throwing himself sideways.

The bullet plowed ground directly beneath the belly of the big dappled colt. Like all green-broke young horses, he was as limber as a snake and subject to unexpected and violent eruptions. He blew apart with a loud snort at the same moment Grant Osborne squeezed his trigger. The bullet tore air where George had been, not where he was after firing, and there was no opportunity for another shot because the big colt sprang into the air, got his head down, and sunfished. Osborne lost his six-gun and his reins. The big colt bucked, not in a straight line but twisting from side to side. To Osborne's credit, he stayed up there through four back-wrenching pitches, then, as the colt got his head down between his knees and upended, Osborne went through the air, clawing with both hands. He came down in a patch of scabrus rocks that barely showed above the surface of the ground, bounced once and fell back, face down.

Walt's customary imperturbability kept him in place throughout. He watched the colt buck another few yards, then stop to look back. He was rid of the creature on his back, to which he probably attributed that deafening noise and the stinging sensation of sharp pebbles peppering his underside. As soon as the colt halted, Walt looked for George, who was getting to his feet. Their eyes met. "I knew I'd miss if I fired at him," George said apologetically. "And there was only one slug in the little gun. So I thought since he was riding a hackamore colt, if I could frighten the horse Osborne might miss when he shot back."

Walt lifted his hat, settled it again, and looked steadily at George for an extra moment before blowing out a big sigh and shaking his head. "George, you surprise hell out of me every now an' then. I got to hand it to you, partner." Walt spat, hitched up his trousers — his belt was still around Marshal Kandelin's leg — picked up his six-gun, and went over where Osborne was lying.

George was beating dust and dirt off himself when Walt called with a drag in his voice, "George, you better come over here."

Walt moved aside so George could bend down and roll Grant Osborne onto his back. He leaned over him for a moment or two, then sank to one knee and put his fingers against Osborne's neck. George twisted around, and looked up at Walt in disbelief. "He's dead," he said, gently lifting Osborne's head. As he did this, Walt said, "Busted neck?"

George nodded.

Walt went after his Winchester, blew the dirt off it, and shoved it back into the saddle boot. Then he chummed his way up to the dappled colt and led him back. The other horses eyed him with strange-horse curiosity. Walt called over, "If we tie him belly down across his colt, George, we better make a real short checkrein, or the damn horse is going to come apart again."

They actually had no difficulty getting Osborne across his saddle and tying him with his own lariat. Walt made a checkrein of one of Osborne's reins and they started out again —

gingerly for the first mile, watching the colt's every move. But evidently he was one of those animals who behaved best in company. He went along without a bobble. When they were satisfied and had passed the distant rooftops of the Osborne place, Walt gazed over there and soberly said, "There's another piece of land Alvarado can gobble up, if he's crazy enough to want it."

George was thinking along different lines. "If we ride into Lordsville like this, it's going to start tongues wagging like they never wagged before. Your bandage is slipping."

Walt raised a hand to push the gingham cloth back into place and answered drolly, "They'll just have to wag, partner, because I don't know any other place to take these gents. Anyway, Kandelin belongs up there."

CHAPTER 23

REACTIONS

When they entered Lordsville it was early evening, the sidewalks were practically empty and most of the business establishments were closed for the day.

At the livery barn the watery-eyed old scarecrow of a night man greeted them without seeming to be breathing. He leaned on a manure fork to watch them unload the two dead men, one of whom the old man knew very well, having been thrown into his cells a number of times when he had appeared in public with a load on.

He would not go any closer than the lower part of the runway, not even when Dr. Brunner offered the reins of their horses. The old man said, "Just tie 'em, gents. I'll get to them in a few minutes. . . . You fellers look pretty strange."

Walt fingered his gingham bandage and nodded. "Feel pretty strange too, partner. By the way, is Henry Stoll around?"

The old man raised a soiled cuff to mop at watering eyes. "Now then, mister, you know he ain't. He's up at Doc Homer's place on a plank in the back shed. Some Mexicans brought him in this afternoon in a wagon. An' folks know what happened to him. One of you gents shot him."

Walt looked annoyedly at the blunt hostler. "And do they know why we shot him?"

"Yes. Mr. Alvarado got the whole story. He passed it around. I'll tell you flat out, gents, I never liked Henry. He bullied me somethin' fierce. I won't be one of his pallbearers, but around town there's a heap of wondering. 'specially after Marshal Kandelin run for it, and Mr. Goldsmith an' his clerk from the emporium got convinced by Mr. Alvarado to tell their story at the jailhouse. Somethin' like this just plain gets folks chasin' their tails. As far back as I know, nothin' like it's ever happened in Lordsville before."

George nudged Walt. They left the old man to look after their animals and crossed to the café. There were no other diners; the regular patrons had eaten supper an hour or so earlier.

The café man took root behind his counter — it would almost have been possible to sit astraddle one eyeball and saw off the other one the way he stared in absolute speechlessness.

George leaned on the counter and said, "Water. Five glasses each."

The café man turned without a word and walked stiffly in the direction of his kitchen. When he returned, most of the shock had worn off. He put two pitchers of water on the counter with two glasses, and as his patrons drank he said, "Where's the marshal?"

Walt jerked his head. "Down at the livery barn." He drank more water, looking steadily at the café man. "Dead. What do you have for supper?"

The café man swallowed hard before answering. "Antelope steak with potatoes and coffee."

George looked up. "Is that antelope steak flat or round?"

The café man's pale brows dropped a notch. "Flat. There ain't any such things as round antelope steak."

George reached for his third glass of water.

The meal was excellent — not by all standards perhaps, but by the standards of two men who hadn't eaten in a long time. They left the café feeling like bloated toads. Night was down, there was noise coming from the saloon, which was northward a few doors, and over at the corral yard, where a late day stage had just arrived, men were moving around with lanterns.

George jerked his head for Walt to follow him. Walt trooped along without asking where they were going. When George turned in past Homer Hudspeth's sagging little picket gate, Walt said, "Maybe we could get some plain white cloth for my face."

Inside, Homer was sitting in the parlor with his glasses halfway down his nose, reading a book. He looked up so suddenly the glasses fell to the floor. George nodded. "It's been a long day, Homer. We could use a shot of your popskull."

As Doctor Hudspeth struggled up out of the chair he narrowly missed stepping on his glasses. He led the way to the kitchen, where he turned and said, "Where in the hell have you been?"

Walt answered. "Hunting down the town marshal. We brought him back belly down. And another scoundrel, a man named Grant Osborne. You got objections to pouring us a drink?"

Homer didn't move. "George, did you put that bandage on him? It looks like part of a lady's dress."

"It was. Her skirt. Homer, we could use some of your special whiskey."

Doctor Hudspeth turned ponderously toward his whiskey cupboard. As he reached inside he said, "What in the hell has been going on? Alvarado and his riders have been intimidating the town since Frank Kandelin ran off. They got Goldsmith and his clerk at the jailhouse, and I've got Henry Stoll in the back shed, dead as a stone."

Walt and George pulled out chairs and sat down, saying nothing as they watched Homer fill three glasses. George nodded and reached for his glass. "I killed Stoll," he raised the glass slightly in Walt's direction. "To being alive," he said. They downed their whiskey and put the glasses aside. Walt reached up to untie and remove his bandage. Homer turned up the kitchen lamp and George stared. The holes in Barnard's cheeks were healed. There were no scabs. The flesh looked pink and tender, but healed. George was too dumbfounded to speak, but Homer was not. He leaned to gently examine the wounds. "They look fine," he said, and leaned back to pick up his glass of whiskey. "When did it happen — four, five weeks back?"

Walt very gently scratched his face where it itched and looked sardonically at George Brunner. "You want to tell him?" he asked.

293

George looked into his glass before speaking. "It happened day before yesterday, Homer."

Hudspeth put down the glass he had been raising. "That's not much of a joke," he said, and started to raise the glass again.

"It is not a joke, Homer. Stoll shot him through the face day before yesterday."

Homer put the glass down, rose and lifted the lamp to hold it close and examine the wounds. "Five weeks ago at the least," he announced and sat back down. He fixed George with a level scowl. "You want to start at the beginning, or do you want to wash and shave first?"

George yawned. "Maybe in a day or two. Right now I want a bath and ten hours of sleep. So does Walt. Can we put him up?"

Homer nodded, still scowling faintly. "Yes. On the cot in the examination room. George . . . you shot Henry Stoll?"

"Yes. In Maria Antonia Lord's bedroom. It was Stoll who tried to kill her the day of her father's funeral."

"Stoll? Why?"

George sighed. "Maybe tomorrow or the next day. How was Father O'Malley's funeral?"

It was a diversion and it worked. Homer refilled his glass and pushed the bottle toward the center of the table, in case either of the younger men was interested. Neither of them was. "I never saw so many people at a burial before," he exclaimed. "They came from all directions. A priest came down from up north somewhere to do the honors. . . . George, I'd just as soon not talk about it. Come along, we'll get Mr. Barnard fixed up with fresh blankets and all."

The three men rose, but only Walt followed Homer out of the kitchen. George remained behind. He put the tub on the stove, fed wood into the firebox, and went to haul water from the well out back to fill the tub with. It was hard work, and he had not been uplifted by the whiskey. If anything, it made him more weary and drowsy. But that may have been caused by the water they had drunk at the café and the big meal they had eaten down there.

He was shedding filthy clothing when Homer appeared in the doorway. "That is just not possible," he exclaimed, scowling darkly. "Walt Barnard told me what the woman did for his wounds. It simply is not possible."

George nodded. "You're right, Homer. See you in the morning — and don't rattle my door before noon."

Hudspeth fidgetted. He wanted to stay, but George turned his back, so the older man went off to his own bedroom.

The bath made a world of difference, and when George shaved afterward he felt even better. He had just finished emptying the tub out back when Walt came into the kitchen. Homer had daubed both his cheeks with oily ointment. There would always be scars, but the wounds looked better than any physician would have expected them to look. They altered the bronzed rangeman's appearance only very slightly.

George offered to help haul water for Walt's bath, and Walt accepted, not because he was too tired to do it by himself but because there were some things on his mind he wanted to discuss.

As they brought in the buckets and waited for the tub to get hot, Walt said, "If I wasn't worn down to the bone, I'd go over to Mex town."

George was understanding. "As pretty and nice as she is, I'd go even if I was tired. She's certainly heard a lot and has worried." He grinned. "You're a lucky man, but I'll be damned if I understand what she sees in you."

Walt grinned back. "That'll be a healthy sign, George. I'd have been a lot more uncomfortable ridin' around with you if you'd felt otherwise. Where's the soap?"

George took it from beneath a towel and

pitched it over. The fugitive caught it. "You know, she's the main reason I went with you after Kandelin," he said. "She'd never be safe in a town run by a lawman gone bad. She grew up around here. She's got friends on both sides of Main Street. And her uncle is here."

"What are you getting at?"

"I hate to take her away from here. She'll go, but it don't seem right to do it."

"Then don't," George responded, emptying the last of the water into the tub and chucking more wood into the firebox.

Walt sat down. "You're right. I won't take her away. But sayin' good-bye is goin' to hurt like hell."

George turned and stared. "What are you talking about? You told me you liked Lordsville. . . . Is it the dodger?"

"Yeah. Sooner or later someone will come along, George."

George thought that was probably true, but he was not in the mood for a prolonged discussion, so he slapped Walt roughly on the shoulder and went off to bed.

Sleep arrived quickly and was of the deep variety that usually accompanies complete physical exhaustion. He did not even waken when the early morning stagecoach went rattling northward up out of town, or when several barking dogs raised Cain over across the road on the east side of town.

Someone down at the blacksmith's shop was warping steel over an anvil, and even that did not stir him. When George's eyes finally opened it was a thought, not the town noises, that roused him. He did not move, except to raise his glance from the sunshine coming through his roadside window to the white ceiling.

It was, he told himself, gratitude and nothing more that had influenced the beautiful woman to say she was fond of him. Women were emotional. In a mood of tremendous relief, thankfulness, and reaction to what appeared to them as some form of deliverance, they would offer an emotional response — affection.

Hell! He sat up and looked around. A month from now they would be back to "Dr. Brunner" and "Señorita Lord."

Homer rattled the door, then poked his head in. George stared at him. Homer did not offer a greeting, he simply said. "Walt and I are having ham and eggs," and closed the door.

George searched for his clean britches and began dressing. Someone pounded on the front door. He ignored it. Homer's voice sounded resonantly and the door was closed. George headed through the kitchen for the wash house out back, nodding to Walt and wrinkling his nose at the pleasant aromas in the kitchen. When he returned, Homer and Walt were eating. Homer looked up, showing irritation. "Everyone knows you and Walt are back. They know what you left down at the livery barn, and tongues are wagging. That was Jeff Morgan from the harness works at the door just now. He's head of the town council this year. He wants to talk to you."

George sat down and speared a slab of ham. "What about?"

"Kandelin, of course. And other things."

George and Walt exchanged a look. "They have to bury Frank and the other man, Grant Osborne, and they have to get another marshal appointed. And when we get around to it, we'll talk to them, but not today and maybe not tomorrow."

Walt nodded as he chewed, eyes fixed on the far wall. Homer considered them both briefly and went back to his meal. George, who usually was very observant, did not notice that the first time in a couple of years, they were having breakfast in the kitchen and Homer did not pour whiskey into his coffee.

After eating, Walt left the house without saying when he would return. Homer, who was beginning to accept the fact that neither of the younger men was going to tell him what happened until they were damn good and ready, shrugged as George left him to clean up the kitchen. He was only halfway through when the white-faced townsman came to breathlessly insist Homer accompany him down to his residence. His wife was having a difficult labor. George's bedroom door was open. He heard every word, including Homer's final one as he went for his hat and satchel.

"Babies!"

George smiled to himself, studied his face in a wavey glass mirror, and was mildly surprised at what he saw. His face was almost as tanned as Walt's. His cheeks were less fleshy than they had been, his eyes were different too; they appeared to be less idealistic, more fatalistically mature. Their direct gaze reflected a new depth. He was not sure he liked what he saw, so he went after his hat. Ten minutes later when he left the house, he encountered Don Carter Alvarado out at the hitching post in front of the house. Alvarado had just arrived; he looked around while tying his horse and George nodded to him. Alvarado nodded back, "Did you get him?" he asked.

George nodded again. They would only be talking about Marshal Kandelin. "Yes, we got him."

"We? Walt Barnard and you?"

"Yes."

"Where is Walt?"

George gave a delayed response. "He had some business to take care of. He'll be along directly."

"I heard he got shot out at the Lord place."

"By Henry Stoll. And Stoll is dead. Homer's got him back in the embalming shed."

"Good. Then you two got out there in time. How is Señorita Lord?"

"When I saw her last she looked very well. That's where I'm headed just now."

Carter Alvarado studied Dr. Brunner for a moment before speaking again. "You've been here long enough to know this country fairly well, Doctor. When the Indians were still troublesome it was said they learned things very swiftly by what people called their 'moccasin telegraph.' Now, the Mexicans call it by a different name, but it means the same thing."

George waited for the rest of it.

"Doctor, some of my riders are related to some of the people out at the Lord place. I heard two weeks ago that Maria Antonia has grown very fond of you."

George shrugged. "Gratitude, Mr. Alvarado. It's common in my business."

But Alvarado gently shook his head, dark

301

eyes as steady as stones. "No, I don't think so, Doctor. It's more than that." He paused. "Well, I wish you well." Before George could speak again Carter Alvarado turned to untie the reins holding his animal to the hitching post and said, "Come back when you can. Meanwhile, I'm going to try and organize the town, get someone appointed to serve the rest of Kandelin's term as town marshal, and send a rider to hunt down the circuit riding judge so we can try the remaining conspirators. And, George . . . tell her — I know I behaved badly. She'll know what I mean. Tell her that someday I want to ride over. And whatever she does, I wish her well."

George watched the handsome rancher mount and turn southward down Main Street. As he watched he speculated to himself that Alvarado was one of those people who moved in and took charge when the need arose. He would do as he had just said, he would contribute to the restoration of order. Maybe the reason old David Lord had not liked Carter Alvarado was that they were too much alike.

The doctor started southward toward the livery barn, and although several people would have intercepted him, he avoided them all, except one. Jeff Morgan stood with crossed arm as erect as a soldier in the doorway of his saddle and harness shop. He and George had met often, but never professionally because Jeff Morgan did not believe much in physicians, and because George owned no harness that required repairing.

The older man blocked George's southward walk. "Two things I want to know, Doctor," he said. "The first one is, who shot Marshal Kandelin?"

George eyed the big old rawboned man. "Why do you want to know that, Jeff?"

"Because if it was you, then the town council's got a problem on its hands. If it was that feller who rides for Alvarado, well then maybe we don't have a problem. We need a new marshal."

George asked, "What's the second question?"

"Easier than the first, Doctor. You rode with the cowboy huntin' Frank down. Would you say he'd make a good replacement for Frank?"

George smiled slightly. "I think he'd make the best town marshal you could get, Jeff."

The harness maker unclasped his big arms and nodded thoughtfully. "I got faith in your judgment. So do most other folks around town." As Morgan stepped aside he dropped his voice and said, "I got that wanted dodger on Barnard in the shop if you want to see it."

George stared. "You took it from the jailhouse office? Why, Jeff?"

"Well, let me put it this way," the older man said, and leaned on the doorjamb. "Twenty years back I done something that was maybe foolish, but that needed doing. Ever since I've had a little understandin' about such things as wanted posters. So I felt that if that feller come back with you after a manhunt, and you still approved of him, I'd burn the poster, recommend him to the council, an' as far as you and me are concerned, there never was a damn poster. All right, Doctor?"

George smiled. "All right, Jeff. He's a lot better man than a damn dodger makes him out to be."

Jeff Morgan's eyes twinkled sardonically. "It happens every now and then. Everyone who's on a dodger ain't worthless."

George gazed at the lined, granite-jawed face with its sunk-set, dead-level gray eyes and dryly said, "Jeff, you're right. I think I know two men who prove you're right. Walt Barnard is one of them."

George winked. Morgan winked back, and as Dr. Brunner continued on southward, the big older man straighted up off his doorjamb to return to his work.

There was a new hostler at the livery barn. George thought he had seen him before but could not remember where, and the day man did not enlighten him. He simply asked if George wanted his sorrel horse.

George didn't. "He's had enough for a while. Rig me out one of the livery horses."

The day man nodded, and said, "Doctor, you don't want to baby 'em, or they get spoilt an' barn-sour and — "

"Seems I recall hearing all this before, friend. Now, about that livery horse . . ."

The day man walked away and returned leading a muscular buckskin horse. He worked in silence, and even after he had rigged out the horse and handed George the reins he did not speak, although he went out to the back alley and watched the doctor mount. Apparently he was one of the those people whose behavior was adversely affected for the rest of the day by even such a slight rebuff as George had given him on the subject of spoiling horses.

There was heat, but it was less noticeable than it had been on other days. George wondered if it was less, or if he had become somewhat more inured to it after his travail on the South Desert.

The land was not shimmering though, so perhaps there actually was less heat. He could see farther too, without visibility being softly obscured by distant heat haze.

The wildflowers were blooming; in some places entire areas of them glowed yellow or red or rusty brown. The air smelled powerfully of their perfume, and the farther George rode, the less he thought of yesterday and the day before. He had killed a man and had contributed to the death of two more men. He had done those things to survive and so that his companion would survive. He had no crisis of conscience, for although he had been trained to nurture life and had done so many times to the best of his ability, he had never believed that all life was precious. Most of it was, but not all of it.

CHAPTER 24

A SOUND OF LAUGHTER

Juan Esteven was struggling to sweat a wagon tire to the wooden wheel. The trick was to put the tire on hot, then shrink it with cold water, but that was only successful providing the steel tire was not wedged on while it was *too* hot; otherwise it made the wood smoulder and char, which ruined the entire wheel.

Good wheelwrights were as scarce as hen's teeth, and ranch blacksmiths who might be entirely competent at shoeing horses or making replacement parts for wagons from forge to anvil rarely had the experience or talent to retire wagon wheels. Juan Esteven was no exception. He had gone through the proper sequences, but only just barely, and now as George walked from the tie rack in front of the barn to the blacksmith shop to watch, Juan looked around with a sweaty, anxious expression and said, "Amigo, do you know anything about this?"

George shook his head. "No. But the wood is smoking, Juan. The steel is too hot." He nodded to the struggling mayordomo and struck out for the big house, its red roof tiles glowing in brilliant sunshine.

The curandera emerged from the patio as Dr. Brunner was reaching for the gate from the opposite side. They were both startled. The doctor recovered first and told her how much he admired the work she'd done on Walt's wounds. Then he did something that startled the old woman — he bent and kissed the curandera on the cheek.

She did not retreat but she seemed poised to, then she smiled and blushed. She offered her dark, work-hardened hand. Dr. Brunner gripped it, and they parted.

There were birds in the shaggy old trees beyond the house, and there was a sound of water running somewhere in the patio as George went to the steel-reinforced oak door. This time when he was admitted it was by the squatty girl with ribbons in her hair, and while her smile was as pleasant as before, there seemed to be more restraint in her gaze as she led him across the parlor. The squatty girl seemed to know instinctively that Señorita Maria Antonia Lord y Gallegos, even at her advanced age of thirty-one, had found what the girl only dreamed of finding, and there was no question of competition, so the girl led George to the bedroom door, knocked lightly, smiled at him, and departed.

Doña Teresa Maria opened the door, erect and with her unsmiling dark eyes as fixed as always. George nodded and stepped past her, pulling off his hat as he did so.

Maria Antonia turned from the grilled window, fully dressed, with her long hair intricately plaited. With the sun at her back and the expression of mixed relief and serenity on her magnificent features, she was so stunning that George caught his breath, but only for seconds. Then he faced her aunt. "Why is she out of bed?" he said.

Teresa Maria, who had never been defensive before, now was. She fluttered her hands and moved toward the foot of the large old bed. She spoke in Spanish. "I can say to you, Doctor, that it has always been so; she is more of her father than her mother — may God grant peace to both their souls."

George looked at the beautiful woman by the window. She seemed to be holding back a smile when she spoke. "It sounds better that way. If she had spoken in English it would have come out that I am too pigheaded to listen."

George moved to the little ladder-back chair and leaned on it. He did not know what to say, so wisely, he said nothing. Maria Antonia walked around the bed toward him and smiled.

"I worried. I was afraid. I could not sleep last night until the curandera gave me cloudy water to drink. . . . George?"

He smiled back. "It's finished, I hope. Walt Barnard and I brought Marshal Kandelin back. There was some unpleasantness. I'll tell you about it someday. Don Alvarado has taken charge in town."

She nodded, murmuring a thought. "Yes, and he will do what is best. If there is one thing Carter does well, it is organize and dominate."

George let that pass. "He sends you his best wishes in whatever you do, and his apologies for being angry with you. He said he will ride over when he can."

Her interest was not in Carter Alavardo. "Were you injured?"

"No. Neither was Walt. We got pretty thirsty, though, before we got back. . . . Maria, what will it take to make you stop believing you are fully recovered?"

Her eyes wavered for the first time and Doña

Teresa Maria, who had been standing with both hands clasped over her stomach, made a slight sniffing tone of disapproval. "It is impossible to talk to her sometimes," she told George.

She was ignored. George had to make an effort to pull his gaze away from the beautiful woman. He cleared his throat and studied the rawhide seat of the ladder-back chair. "We could go to the patio; the weather is warm, there is no wind . . ." Maria Antonia said softly.

George continued to stare at the chair seat for a moment, then looked up nodding. "Briefly." He was satisfied that her recovery was nearly complete and had an errant thought: there must be something in the air of this damn country; people healed faster here than anywhere he had ever been.

They left Doña Teresa Maria in the bedroom and went to the patio. The birds were still up there and someone, probably an exasperated mayordomo, was beating steel with a maul across the yard. Distantly, a small child was crying, and equally as distant, someone was playing a guitar. The song was one of those dolorous paeans that had probably come out of Africa with the Moors and, after a seven-hundred-year occupation of Iberia, had become the folk music of Spain, to be transplanted to Spain's New World *encomiendos*. George had heard this particular song so many times he knew most of the words. The song told the story of a beautiful *mestizo* girl whose lover had ridden away with one of the early expeditions of exploration and had never returned, and of a scheming father who insisted that she marry a rich merchant of Veracruz twice her age and leeringly lecherous. She had wept torrents of tears and had prayed her beads for two years, then had married the older man. Her lover never did return, and she died of grief six months after her wedding.

Maria Antonia raised her face and breathed in a great sweep of the fragrant, warm air. George was fascinated by her beauty — and was clinically interested in how deeply she had drawn her breath. She caught his look and laughed. He did not believe he had ever heard her laugh before. They went to a weathered old bench worked out of tough juniper by some long-gone artisan. Trees shaded that part of the patio. The overhead birds fled.

Maria Antonia said, "I owe you my life."

He did not think so. "I understand your father had the constitution of a horse, Maria. You inherited it."

"I didn't mean that."

He looked up quickly. "Stoll?"

She was slow to reply. "I suppose for

312

keeping him from killing me. But . . . for being my doctor and – "

"You don't owe me anything. Maria?"

"Yes."

He did not want to destroy this moment and he did not want to speak brutally, but he had to take the risk. He said, "Any medical man will tell you that gratitude from a patient is a source of discomfort to him. I'm telling you this because I don't want anything like that between us. I am in love with you. I told you that – Maria, don't be grateful."

Her dark eyes went to his face and remained there. They had a hint of testiness in them. Her voice was soft as she replied. "George, everyone is grateful for something. It's our nature, isn't it? But . . ." Her eyes wavered and color rose in her cheeks. "This is hard for me, and you haven't made it any easier." She drew in another big breath and said, "I am in love with you." Then, as though to rush past this announcement, she added, "It's not gratitude. It's something else. . . ." Her color was still high as she went on. "I watched your expression as you listened to the guitar player. You don't like our music."

"Wait a minute," he said quickly. "It's not that I don't like it, Maria, it's just that the songs are so damn sad."

"Not all of them." She studied his face. "The country, the way we live — most things are very different."

He unconsciously raised a hand to gently stroke his jaw. He had an urge to grin but didn't. "Different, yes, but I do like the country and I'm learning to like everything else — even the way of life."

She said, "Curanderas?"

Now he did grin, and he laughed. "Maria, your curandera did something Homer wouldn't believe. In two days she healed Walt Barnard's face. Homer couldn't have done it in six months. No medical doctor could have. On my way in today I met her. We are friends. As for the chicken entrails and clay, they aren't my way, but if they work I'm not going to sit in judgment."

She relaxed on the bench, and smiled. "If you married me, would it work out for us? Would it last?"

His eyes jumped across the patio to that eroded section of mud wall where her bushwhacker had probably fired from. This was the damnedest conversation he had ever been part of. One moment he felt desperately in love, and next moment she showed mild annoyance with him, and then he wanted to laugh. And none of those emotions were light ones. They went deep.

He turned toward her slowly. "Did it last between your father and mother? They were different, weren't they?"

She did not answer the question. "My mother and aunt told me that marriage is something to work at. If people will do that, it will last. My aunt even said it will get better and keep getting better. Do you know how old I am, George?"

He thought he knew, but he had more tact than to answer honestly. "Young enough to survive a gunshot wound that would have killed some people."

"Thirty-one. Isn't that too old for children?"

He stared at her, then made a sweeping gesture toward the jacals, which were not visible from the patio. "How many women over there have children at forty, and even fifty?"

She was silent for a long time. Then she said, "But you don't ask me, George."

"Children?" he said, slightly confused.

She reddened again. "No . . . My God, at times men are so thick!"

"Oh. Maria, will you marry me?"

Her face brightened. Her expression seemed to reflect a variety of serenity, as though something had just arrived in her life that she had almost given up believing would ever arrive. "Yes."

She turned, and he leaned to brush her lips with his mouth. The clarion ring of someone hammering steel had ceased without his being aware of it. The birds had returned, too, and that noise also went unnoticed.

He said, "Your aunt will have a fit."

Maria Antonia shook her head. "No, she won't. She likes you. Not at first, but that's always been her way. Now she doesn't think there is anyone like you." At the look of doubt on his face she laughed. "My aunt . . . is my aunt. She doesn't smile or relax very often."

"She smiled for me, Maria."

"Yes. She told me. I think you are the only man since her husband died who has made her smile. She has had her religion. I'm glad she has it. Give her a little time, George."

They sat in fragrant shade talking quietly of many things, until she suddenly said, "What will you tell Dr. Hudspeth?"

He nodded without responding immediately, because that was something to think about. "I don't know, Maria. He can find another associate, I suppose."

"George, I never wanted to succeed my father as patrón. You've been down here long enough, you know what we are like. We value family, children. I was almost ready to believe these things would never happen to me. It makes a woman lose the desire to laugh, to smile, to even dream. With you, I could laugh. Will you be patrón of Lord's Land?"

He puffed out his cheeks and expelled the breath slowly, which made her laugh at him.

"Don't look so worried," she said, and he gazed at her.

"When I rode in Juan was trying to fit a steel tire to a wagon wheel. He asked if I knew anything about that, I had to say that I didn't. The same goes for the rest of it — the cattle, the business of ranching."

"Are you too old to learn?"

"Well, probably not."

"For me, would you try?"

He smiled and reddened at the same time. "For you, I'd try to reach the moon."

She rose from the bench. "Will you come with me and tell my aunt you asked me to marry you and that I accepted?"

He rose more slowly than she had. "You could tell her," he said.

She made a small exasperated gesture. "George, it is the custom. . . . But all right, we'll both tell her."

He accompanied her back inside. In his mind he had a vision of Doña Teresa Maria drawing herself up, with both hands clasped across her flat stomach, and looking expressionlessly at him from black and unsmiling eyes.

It seemed that his premonition was correct. Doña Teresa Maria was standing just inside the door when they entered, erect, hands clasped. Since her patron saint probably would not have approved of her leaving the door ajar so that she had heard every word that had passed between them on the bench, she was expressionless when they faced her.

George smiled. Tía Teresa Maria did not smile back. He took a shallow breath and met the stone-steady black eyes. Of course there were the preliminaries to any serious discussion, which he had learned over the past two years were dear to the heart of *gachupines,* but for the life of him he could not think of how to begin, so he spoke as a norte americano. He simply said, "Doña Teresa Maria, I asked your niece to marry me, and she accepted."

There was a long moment of silence, as though the older woman were waiting for more, but there was no more. She looked at her niece, who almost imperceptibly inclined her head and Teresa Maria unclasped her hands, relaxed her stance, and moved close and kissed George on the cheek. Then she brought forth a tiny wisp of linen, raised it to her face, and fled from the room.

George looked after her, and because he was

sure he had absolutely shattered the older woman's world, he made a little flapping gesture with both arms and turned a pained look on the beautiful woman beside him.

She laughed at his expression, felt for his hand, and squeezed it. "She is happy, George."

"Really?"

She tugged at his hand. "Now don't be a doctor. I want to walk. I want to go across the yard. I want to hold your hand as we talk."

He turned to hold the door for her. They crossed the patio to the big, sunbright yard, and he felt for her hand as they moved clear of the big house. As they walked he had an inkling about what they were doing and asked quietly if this were some kind of ritual.

She held back the laughter this time. "Yes. By evening everyone on the ranch will know. We don't tell them and they don't ask. This is how it's done. Is that all right?"

He smiled. "I think it's a wonderful idea."

She squeezed his fingers.

THORNDIKE PRESS HOPES you have enjoyed this Large Print book. All our Large Print titles are designed for the easiest reading, and all our books are made to last. Other Thorndike Press Large Print books are available at your library, through selected bookstores, or directly from the publisher. For more information about current and upcoming titles, please call us, toll free, at 1-800-223-6121, or mail your name and address to:

THORNDIKE PRESS
P. O. BOX 159
THORNDIKE, MAINE 04986

There is no obligation, of course.

DM

E,